Damon Runyon's Boys

BY MICHAEL SCOTT CAIN

STARK HOUSE

Stark House Press • Eureka California

DAMON RUNYON'S BOYS

Published by Stark House Press
1315 H Street
Eureka, CA 95501
griffinskye3@sbcglobal.net
www.starkhousepress.com

ISBN-13: 978-1-944520-45-8

Book design by Mark Shepard, SHEPGRAPHICS.COM
Proofreading by Bill Kelly

First Stark House Press Edition: April 2018

FIRST EDITION

Michael Scott Cain Bibliography

Fiction:

Jason's Song (1974)

False Starts, Sudden Stops (1979)

What the Night Will Bring (1995)

Midnight Train (2003)

Arbuckle's Dance (2014)

Non-Fiction:

Co-op Publishing Handbook (1978)

Book Marketing: An Intelligent Guide to Book Distribution (1981)

The Community College in the Twenty-First Century:
A Systems Approach (1999)

The Americana Revolution: From Country and Blues Roots
to the Avett Brothers, Mumford & Sons, and Beyond (2017)

1

The two shooters were identically dressed—wide shoulders, big lapels on zoot suits with coats that were too long and tightly pegged trousers. They wore snap brimmed hats. Dressed this way, the taller one felt like a fool and took no comfort at all in the fact that most of the guys who passed him on the street were dressed the same way. Jesus, at this point in his life, he was running around dressed like some kind of uptown viper? He just felt stupid. The fact that they were uptown, in Harlem, standing right in front of the Savoy Ballroom where all of the dancers wore these outfits didn't help at all.

"When we go in," he told his partner, "we just walk up front like we own the place…"

"People are going to see us."

"Of course, people are going to see us. That's the beauty of it. Everybody sees us, nobody notices us."

"That doesn't make any sense."

Breaking in a new recruit was always a job. These people didn't know the first thing. "Look," he said. "There's a thousand people in there. Nobody's going to notice anything about us. First off, they're going to be focusing on the show, not us." He grinned, pleased to play the role of the old veteran, the guy who *knew*. Fact was, he was a good teacher. "After we do it, they're going to be screaming, running for their lives. Nobody's going to be paying any attention to you and me."

"You've done this before."

"That's a fact."

"So I guess you know how it goes."

The older man's voice tightened a little. "And in just a few minutes, you'll know, too."

"Yeah. Okay. If you're sure…"

"I am. Now, here's what you're going to do. We're going in. When he comes out, you walk up to him—I'll be right beside you—shove your piece into his gut and empty it out into his body. It's that simple."

"You know, I sort of wish we didn't have to do this."

"I know. Everybody feels that way. But we have to do it." He grinned once more. "Ready?"

"Ready."

"Let's go in."

"Damon," Linda said, still watching a couple in front of her, "Can I ask you a question?"

Taylor scribbled in his notebook. After finishing his sentence, he put the cap back on his pen and said, "Sure. What's on your mind?"

"If you don't intend to dance with me," she twirled her hair around her fingers, "Why are we here?"

Her red hair was pulled up into a bun that fit under a black hat that had flowers on it. Taylor didn't understand the hat, but then, he thought, the list of things he didn't understand about women's fashion was endless. So was the list of things he didn't know about Linda.

"Linda, you know I'm not what you'd call a light on my feet. Last time I danced was back before the war, at my editor's wedding. He still blames my fox trot for the divorce."

"Then maybe you can tell me what we're doing here?" She reached for her pack of Chesterfields, began to shake one out, but then changed her mind.

"I'm working, darling," he said.

A couple executed a quick series of spins in front of them, culminating in the man rolling the woman across his back. He looked at Taylor and Linda as though he expected applause.

"Working?" Linda said. "In a dance hall? I never realized *Crime Scene* covered Lindyhop dancing. You're a crime reporter. Lindy-hopping is stupid, sure, but it isn't criminal."

"I'm on a story," he said.

"In the Savoy? Why'd you bring me if you're working. Not that I can see you doing anything that looks like work."

"Hell, lady, weren't you saying just a little earlier in the evening that you didn't have anything to do tonight?" he said. "I thought you'd enjoy being here, that's all."

Linda lived upstairs from Taylor. They'd met the day she'd moved in, about three months earlier. He'd come home from the office and found her trying to wrestle an armchair up the stairs. After helping her carry her stuff into the apartment, he took her out for dinner and they'd become friends over the meal.

"I understand," she said. "You thought I'd enjoy coming to the biggest dance hall in the city, listening to the finest music you can hear anywhere on earth, music so fabulous that it makes it impossible to sit still, and be the only woman in the place sitting here all by myself, not dancing? You thought I'd get a big kick out of watching everybody but me have fun?"

"Well, I got to admit it isn't working out quite the way I'd figured."

Now she lit the cigarette. Flashing Taylor a disgusted look, she turned and scanned the dancers. A young guy with a number on his back lost control of his partner as he slid her between his legs. She slid out of his hands and crashed into another couple knocking them down like bowling pins…

"Now, that I enjoyed," Linda said.

Brownie Hobson didn't have any idea who or what he was praying to. He'd never been inside a church in his life, had no religious background and was pretty sure he'd never once in his entire life thought about anything that had anything to do with God. All he knew was that before you went on stage, you were supposed to gather in a circle, stack your hands in the center and say a quick prayer as though the Almighty had nothing better to do than make sure a dance act went over well.

Assuming there was an Almighty, of course.

After the prayer, he looked out through the curtain. Like it was every night, the place was jammed. Since the end of the war the whole damn city had gone crazy—years of pent up need for fun had broken through. Most of the action seemed to take place in the dance halls. Every one in the city was jammed each night and for a while there had seemed to be a new one opening every night. Still, the Savoy led the pack. It always had.

The Savoy's dance floor was bigger than a football field—it covered a full city block—and every inch of it was packed with the swing kids and jitterbugs, who provided the show. The spectators, who served as the audience, crowded around the edges of the dance floor to watch the action.

Even though it was only ten p.m., the Savoy was packed. Big Joe Turner and his band were on the raised double stage at the far end of the room and the floor was so packed that the dancers barely had room to execute their maneuvers, which were as complicated and precise as ballet. Young hepcats in pegged and draped zoot suits and porkpie hats tossed around girls in swirling skirts. If a couple was really hot, a group of spectators would gather around them, shouting encouragement and clapping out the rhythm as they watched.

Brownie Hobson had watched the rise of swing and when he saw it refuse to fade, lingering in the city like a bad smell in a tenement hall, he formed Brownie's Lindy Hoppers to play all the clubs and dance halls that had emerged as competition for the Savoy. The group did big over-rehearsed acrobatic versions of the Lindy where the guys threw the girls around like footballs and they all shouted gleefully and clapped for each other and cheered each other on as if they were worshipers at a revival. Even Brownie knew it was silly as hell, but he also knew he made a good living with it.

He let the curtain fall closed. "Come on, kids," he said, "Let's get out there and kill."

"I ever tell you why it's called the Lindy Hop?" Taylor said.

Linda played with a match stick, wearing her boredom like a masquerade costume. "No."

"One night in 1927, right after Lindbergh crossed the ocean, a reporter asked one of the regulars, Shorty George Snowden, what they called the dance he was watching. Shorty George's eyes caught a headline on a discarded paper on a table: *Lindy Hops the Atlantic*.

"'It's called the Lindy Hop,' he said. The name stuck."

"I can't tell you how fascinating that is." She broke the match stick in half and let the pieces fall from her fingers.

The two shooters lingered at the edge of the dance floor. The leader pointed. "We'll make our way around here, get close to the stage. When he comes out, boom."

"That's all there is to it? Boom?"

"Just follow my lead."

They began working their way around the crowd. As he led the way, the leader felt the old energy rise within him and wondered exactly when he'd come to love this work so much.

As Big Joe's outfit walked offstage for their break, Taylor stood and said, "Got to go talk to a couple of people. Be back in a minute."

"I can't wait," Linda sighed.

Turning to a fresh page in his notebook, he walked across the floor to get closer to the stage. The backup band started up and the tuxedoed emcee, after demanding a big round of applause for them, introduced the specialty act, Brownie's Lindy Hoppers. A group of four couples sprinted onto the stage and began dancing as if they were never going to be fed again unless they won this crowd over. The men wore tight black pants and shiny white shirts with sleeves wide enough to hide drugs in. The crowds blocked Taylor's line of sight but he didn't care. The Lindy Hoppers had been around forever and he'd never been able to work up any enthusiasm for them or their work. People who did the Lindy Hop for a living? God, who could possibly give a damn? What kind of person made a decision to become a professional Lindy Hopper?

The house band played loud, doing their own little unison moves, the guys in the horn section executing a complex set of steps and movements as they blasted out a series of choruses. The crowd around the Lindy Hoppers cheered and yelled so loudly that it took a few seconds for everyone to realize that the other noise they heard, the one that wasn't music or shoes with metal taps slamming onto a wood floor or people cheering, was a series of gunshots.

Brownie Hobson stopped dancing, looked down and saw blood spreading across his chest and stomach. He had a shocked expression on his face as he sank to the floor, clutching his stomach.

He looked as though he were staring at the crowd, wondering who among the thousands had turned against him, watching the audience break and run, screaming in panic, for the doors. As the sound of the screaming rose, Hobson collapsed like a punctured tire.

2

"You see this happen, Taylor?" Lieutenant McCall said.

Horace McCall wore a blue serge suit with a tie that was the same shade of red as his face. The tie had what looked like a mustard stain on it. Because McCall was no more than five-seven, Taylor looked down on him and had the same thought he always had: catch a glance of McCall on the street, you'd think he was a salesman in a luggage store. Maybe that's what made him a good cop. Because of his appearance, everybody—bad guys, other cops, reporters—underestimated him. Since he'd been bumping into the man doing stories for *Crime Scene*, Taylor had learned not to make that mistake.

Since they both worked the major crimes, Taylor dealt with McCall just about every day and even if his dealing with the cop didn't always go that smoothly—McCall wasn't the easiest person to get along with—Taylor liked and respected him. The detective was smart, incisive, and relatively honest. Like all good cops, he'd empty out a corpse's billfold and if some quick and easy cash came his way that he could take without compromising his sense of values, he'd pocket it, but he'd bust your ass if you offered him a bribe. His best aspect, though, from Taylor's point of view, was that he always made a good interview.

What more could you ask out of a homicide guy?

They were standing on the dance floor in front of the stage. Being in the Savoy when no music was playing, nobody was dancing, and the house lights were turned up was like being in an empty airport hanger late at night. Without the dancers stirring up the temperature, the room was cold. The air conditioning system's motors rumbled steadily in the background.

Brownie Hobson still lay on the floor, a tan blanket tossed over him. His right hand flopped on the floor, uncovered, palm upward, fingers curled as though he were reaching for a drink. Taylor watched McCall's men work what was left of the crowd, interrogating the dancers who hadn't been able to fight their way through the crush of bodies dashing for the doors. The cops treated the dancers as though they had them in a Q & A room down at the precinct. At the edge of the floor, a circle of uniformed patrolmen held the crowd in place. Taylor wondered absently what they expected to learn from the people who'd been too stunned and slow to make it out during the stampede for the exits.

A couple of hundred members of the audience lingered on the dance floor. They stood silently in small clumps. A dozen or so regulars, off at the far edge of the crowd, worked the room as though they were out visiting neighbors. Off to the right, a couple of hepcats practiced their moves to music they heard in their heads.

Even though he was holding people in the room, McCall had let Linda go home. Taylor had put her in a cab and come back inside.

"I said," McCall repeated, "did you see this happen?"

"I was here," Taylor said, "but I didn't see anything. I'm not sure anybody really saw very much. The crowd was too thick and it happened too fast. All I can tell you is somebody started shooting, Brownie was hit and the place went berserk."

"Then you can't say what exactly happened?"

Taylor shrugged. "The Lindy Hoppers take the floor, the crowd's all gathered around them and halfway through their first number, shots start ringing out. People start running like madmen, heading for the exits. By the time I get up front, Hobson's dead on the floor and everybody's cleared out. I figure the shooter ran out with the crowd."

"I suppose you're going to be writing about this?"

"That's up to Lou Marsczyk."

McCall pushed his hat back. "Hell, you're going to be writing about it. I can't imagine Marsczyk not putting you on the story. You got a celebrity shooting in the Savoy, any one of a thousand people could be the shooter, Christ, even I can see the story's a beauty. The papers are going to be on it like a trick or treater on candy."

One of McCall's men walked over and hovered by his side, waiting to be noticed. McCall ignored him. His cigar had gone out. Relighting it required some effort. When he was satisfied that it was going, he took a puff, then held the cigar out and stared at its burning tip.

"You don't usually worry about what the papers are doing," Taylor said. "What are you telling me here, Lieutenant?"

McCall noticed the man next to him and shot him a glance that told him to be patient, to keep on waiting. Holding his hat in his hands in front of him like a supplicant, the cop backed off a step.

"I'll tell you what's on my mind, Taylor. Newspaper guys are going to swarm all over this place, all over the precinct, they're going to badger everybody and for a day or two, it's going to be Goddamn pandemonium and then, just when they've got everything screwed up real good, they're going to go on to the next scandal and I won't have to worry about them getting in my way anymore. You, though, you're different. You won't leave."

"That good or bad?"

"Depends on your point of view. You're okay, Taylor, and there was a time when you used to be a good reporter, before you got tied up with that damn scandal rag you work for now. You got a good head on your shoulders. But every time you're writing about a case I'm working, it gets weird. You're always there and you got a way of complicating things. That damn rag you write for's going to do what you guys always do. You're going to blow this thing up all out of proportion, make it sound like the grizzliest, most important murder of the fucking century. You're going to blow it up till the whole country's following the case and all that damn attention's going to bring major heat down on me."

"I'll see what I can do about staying out of your way. If I'm assigned to the story, that is."

"You will be, we both know that going in. You got anything I don't have?"

"Not a thing. Told you what little I know."

"How come you happen to be here tonight, anyway? You ain't known far and wide for your dancing feet."

The cop who'd been waiting handed McCall a note. He read it and tucked it in his coat pocket. Taylor wanted to know what it said but knew better than to ask. The only way to get along with McCall—and you weren't going to get a thing out of him if you didn't get along with him—was to sit back and wait for him to let it drop. If he figured you needed it and if it suited his needs for you to have it, he'd share it.

"Doing a story on Big Joe Turner. Nothing to do with Brownie."

The Coroner's guys tossed Brownie's body clumsily onto a stretcher and wheeled it out. His left arm dangled from the stretcher but nobody bothered to lift it. The crowd parted to let them through and closed again behind them. McCall and Taylor watched him go silently.

As the stretcher went through the doors, McCall jerked his head at it. "That's how it ends up, Taylor. I don't give a damn who you are, that's the end of it right there."

Taylor shivered. "Yeah."

Costello's was on 44th Street between Second and Third Avenues. All of the morning paper guys, who spent their nights chasing stories for the midnight deadline hung out there after they had called in their copy and were through for the night. If you were in the neighborhood between stories, you also fell in for a quick one. Taylor loved the place. It was filled with people he knew and understood. On a good night, you could see Ernest Hemingway polish off a steak and a fifth of Rum or you could catch James Thurber doing a cartoon on the walls—all of the editorial cartoonists drew on the walls. During election seasons, you could keep up with a paper's stance by examining Costello's walls. The morning papers had just gone to bed when Taylor walked in, so all of the cityside guys and the crime guys were drinking.

Terry Porter, who covered crime for the *Mirror*, stood at the bar, chatting with a tiny blonde haired kid with thick glasses, who looked like he'd taken notes on how a reporter dressed from prewar Warner Brothers crime movies. He had on a trench coat that he could have picked up by mugging Humphrey Bogart. Whatever Porter was saying, the little guy was taking notes.

"Hey, Terry," Taylor said.

"Well, if it ain't Big Time. Kid, this here's Big Time. Used to work a beat at my paper, back when his name was Damon Taylor. Now you can just call him Big Time. He's got a cushy job at *Crime Scene* magazine, making a fortune, pulling in so much money he can afford to buy the drinks."

"Order it up," Taylor said. He nodded at the kid, who looked like he'd been constructed on a three/quarters scale to a regular person. He was no more than five-three.

"Hi," the kid said. "My name's Capote. Truman Capote. I work for *PM*."

"*PM*, huh?" Taylor said. "Why aren't you out covering a communist party meeting? Reviewing a hootenanny?"

The kid nodded, his chin disappearing behind the upturned collar of his trench coat. "I covered one earlier tonight." His brow furrowed and then he frowned, saying, "Oh, you're kidding me, aren't you?"

"Come on, Big Time, don't give the kid a hard time just because he toes the party line for a Communist paper."

"*PM* isn't communist," the kid explained, his voice earnest. "We're on the left, no question, but it's not communist." He glanced quickly around, checking out the crowd. "Look, with the hearings cranking up in Washington and all, can we go kind of light on the communist talk?"

He had the strangest voice Taylor had ever heard, a southern accented high pitched whisper with a pronounced lilt. He couldn't tell if the kid was camping it up or if that was his real voice. He suspected Capote was putting on the vocal tone. Because the kid's diction was so precise, his words so carefully chosen, the whole effect seemed like something a Broadway actor would work up for a part in a bad play.

"Terry, you hear about Brownie Hobson?" Taylor said.

"Got himself hit over at the Savoy?"

"That's the man."

"Houston's covering it. You got anything?"

Conditioned by the movies, people thought of reporters as Alan Ladd types, hiding everything they knew from everybody else, including the cops and other reporters, charging into the building waving their hats with the press passes in them, shouting, "Stop the presses!" That's the kind of reporter this Capote kid wanted to be, Taylor thought. What the kid was going to have to learn was that the real thing was more complicated. Newsmen helped each other all the time, sharing information, passing along tips. Sure, you wanted to beat your rivals, and when you did every once in a while, you felt great, but just the same you shared information, helped out the guys from the other papers. After all, you all worked in the same business and, since every paper had a different slant, his story wouldn't hurt yours. Just as important was the fact that you built up credits by helping other guys, debts you could call in when you needed to.

"Let's grab a booth," he said.

The Capote kid followed them across the bar to the booths. When Taylor sat down, his hand trailed along the tabletop. It felt rough. Moving his hand, he saw that Jimmy Cannon had carved his name into the wood. The Capote kid arranged his trench coat carefully around him, as if it were a prop, took out his notebook and pen, and looked expectantly across the booth at Taylor.

"You cover crime, Capote?" Taylor said.

The kid flushed. "Well, no, I'm too new for that. I want to, though. I'm working on it. You mind if I listen?"

"What's your beat?"

His flush deepening, Capote said, "General assignment. I'm just starting out. You have to work your way up."

Terry Porter shook his head at the sadness of it all. He was a big man with an acne-scarred face and a belly that hung over his belt. He kept his hat on because he was sensitive about losing his hair. "What do you know about this one, Big Time?"

Johnny Grogan brought a fresh round of drinks to the table. Capote drank his as if it were medicine.

"I was there."

Now Porter brought out his notebook. "Tell me about it."

"Nothing much to tell."

He brought Porter up to date on the case. By the time he'd finished, Harry Laurel from the *Daily News* had joined them. Laurel waited till Taylor stopped talking before he joined in.

"I got a look at the initial report," he said. "Brownie had five slugs in him. Nobody else hit. All those people surrounding him and not a damn soul got hit but him."

"That would suggest a professional hit." Because of his excitement, Capote's voice reached an even higher pitch.

Laurel looked at him as if he were an insect. After a moment, he turned his attention back at the other two men, dismissing the little man. Capote shot him a glance, then looked down at the table.

"He was hit from close up. His clothes were burned by the bullets."

"What kind of slugs?"

"Too early to tell. They'll dig them out at the autopsy tomorrow."

"What angle you pushing?" Porter said.

"The usual," Laurel answered. "Celebrity killing. Maybe a touch of maniac on the loose." He shrugged.

"A little early for maniac on the loose, ain't it?" Porter said.

"Not at my paper."

"I'm not sure it's that simple," Taylor said.

"For the *Daily News* it is. Celebrity killings, it's what people want to read. You know the story."

They did. Except for Capote, each of them had written it in the past.

When Taylor left the bar, Capote hurried out after him. "Mind if I walk along with you?"

"I'm just going crosstown, pick up the Broadway line uptown."

"You live on the West side?"

"West 93rd Street."

"I'm in the Village."

That figured. Capote would be more at home with Bohemians. The kid struck him as a guy in the wrong racket. He was too soft, too refined, for the newspaper life. He was to reporting what Mussolini was to democracy.

"How long you been at *PM?*"

"Just a few months. I haven't been in the city all that long. It's the first paper I've worked on. My first job in the city, in fact."

"Where you from?"

"Alabama."

"What brings you to New York?"

"You don't become a famous writer in Alabama."

"Oh, God, not another one."

"I can't help it. It's what I want to do."

"Capote, let me give you a little advice. Don't stay at *PM* too long. Start hustling for another job now."

"I'm a long way from supporting myself as a writer. I've published a few short stories, but I still have to work. *PM*'s a good place. I'm writing every day. You know, newspaper work didn't hurt Hemingway, did it? Or Ring Lardner."

"Trust me, find yourself a different job."

"Why?"

"*PM* isn't going to last."

"Because of its politics, you mean?"

Editorially, *PM* was in Henry Wallace's pocket and Mike Quill, the labor leader that everybody kept accusing of being a communist, got his best coverage in its pages. Stalin used to get his best press there also, although since the Berlin blockade and the release of the news about the purges, they'd stopped boosting Big Joe so openly. Still, they hadn't renounced their early praise. It wasn't the *Daily Worker*, but it was so far to the left of Hearst's paper, you wouldn't think they both served the same city. As far as newspapers went, it was amateur night. It was the type of rag, Taylor thought, that would hire a green, awkward, odd little kid like Capote and let him call himself a reporter.

"Here's the problem, kid: at *PM*, you got a hundred thousand circulation and it's made up of people who love that old lefty stuff. They just can't get enough stories about labor strife, mistreatment of the Negroes and the Jews, and profiles of folk-singers. You got all the old lefties. Problem is, you don't have anybody else."

"So our readers like what we do. Isn't that good? What's the problem?"

"Problem is in this city you need two hundred thousand to stay afloat and the only way to get that second hundred thousand is to loosen up the paper, widen your focus. But if you do that, you're going to lose the lefties, the only readers you got now. Vicious circle, kid. *PM* won't be able to survive it."

"How do you know all this?"

Since Capote was scurrying to keep up with him, Taylor slowed his pace. He felt like he'd somehow gotten trapped into adopting the kid.

"How do I know it? Journalism's my business, kid. It's what I do."

"Mr. Taylor," Capote said, "this Brownie person. Was he connected?"

"Connected?"

"You know, to organized crime."

"Come on, Capote, he's a guy that swing dances for a living."

They walked across 43rd Street, headed up to Fifth Avenue. The evening was damp and warm and even though it was after midnight, the bars, restaurants and movies still pumped enough people out onto the street to make it crowded.

"The way you said it happened, Mr. Taylor, somebody just opening up on him at point-blank range in front of a thousand people, well, that just makes me think that whoever did it was a member of some organized gang. Maybe Murder Incorporated."

"Kid, in this town, you can hire a killer for fifty bucks and, believe me, they aren't members of any Mafia. Why are you so interested in this anyway? You said yourself crime isn't your beat."

"Oh, I just find murder so fascinating, don't you?" He shivered with delight at the thought of it. "It's just," he paused, either searching for the right word or creating an effect, "so extreme."

Taylor turned left on Fifth Avenue, heading down a block to 42nd Street, where he could pick up the subway uptown. A double-decker bus rolled past them. Capote watched it go by, staring in through the windows. A woman holding a baby sat near the rear of the bus, looking straight ahead.

"Why's she have that kid out so late?" Capote said.

Taylor stopped. Turning to face the little guy, he said, "Capote, you're in the wrong business. Look, you're never going to make it as a crime reporter. You shouldn't even want to. It's a crummy job. What you want to do is get yourself a book advance, write yourself a novel. If that's too far away right now, get yourself set up at a paper that's going to be around a while, get real good at working the society pages. Or maybe do entertainment. That way you can get into doing features, maybe get yourself a column."

"Who do you think I am, Ed Sullivan?"

"Don't say that with some kind of nasty edge in your voice. The guy's got a huge readership, makes a bunch of money, makes his own schedule, working maybe two hours a day tops, and you don't see him hanging around precinct houses and Hell's Kitchen slums all the time."

"But he writes gossip, silly stuff that doesn't mean a damn thing to anybody." Capote shivered again. He seemed to have a different shiver for each emotion. "He writes nightclub news, for Christ's sake. It's all so trivial."

Taylor shook his head. "Wake up, kid. This is a mean life, a dirty life. You don't want to spend all your time wallowing in other people's misery and causing even more people to feel miserable because of the stuff you write. You're not cut out for this life."

When he put it that way, he thought, who was?

3

The next afternoon, Lou Marsczyk called Taylor into his office. When Taylor strolled in, Marsczyk opened his desk drawer and brought out a bottle of scotch. He went back into the drawer for a couple of glasses and filled them almost to the brim. Sliding one across to Taylor, he said, "I understand you were in the house for the Hobson thing. Let's hear it."

When he'd first met Lou Marsczyk, Taylor had wondered how he knew all these things, how he could know who was at an event as soon as it happened. After the first couple of months of working under the guy, though, he quit questioning it and just took it as a given.

"If you saw the morning papers, you know everything I know. Somebody popped Brownie Hobson's balloon at the Savoy last night."

"Happened the way the papers said? Right there on the dance floor? With a thousand witnesses milling around?"

"That's the way it went down, yeah."

"Shooter must have taken forever to get out of the place."

"What do you mean?"

He sipped his scotch. "He couldn't run very fast with a set of balls that size."

Most of the owners of the papers and magazines that used to be concentrated down here in Park Row had left, moving up around midtown into new real estate, taking advantage of the building boom of the thirties to erect their own buildings. Averal Budding hadn't chosen to follow them. He wasn't a man used to following anyone. He owned his Park Row building and published a dozen magazines out of it, everything from hard-boiled pulps to romance rags to a newsweekly that couldn't quite compete with *Time*. *Crime Scene* was the flagship rag and Budding had shown the uncommon good sense to hire Lou Marsczyk, an old line Chicago newsman to run it. "If the man can cover Al Capone, he knows crime," Budding always said.

Marsczyk lived up to what was expected of him. He ran *Crime Scene* as though he and the magazine were a single entity. Each week, he collected and published all the salacious details about the most prominent crimes in the country and, even though Taylor wrote for the rag, he thought it was all about as dignified as a second rate carnival. Every once in a while, he wondered why he stayed here. Most of the time, he pushed the question aside, reminding himself that he had to be somewhere, so why not here. When that didn't work, he took a look at his bank balance. The money was incredible and, as long as he didn't violate deadlines too badly, he made his own hours.

He and Marsczyk sat in easy chairs at the far end of the office. Marsczyk occupied a corner room the size of a night club and acted as though he were the emperor. His clothes were tailored for him on Fifth Avenue and each spring he made a trip to London, at Budding's expense, to have a few suits made on Seville Row. Today, he wore a gray pinstripe in year round wool, a crisply starched white shirt and a gray tie with a pattern of red in it.

"Damn it, Taylor," Marsczyk said, "when are you going to let me take you shopping?"

"Why would I want to do that?"

"Your clothes are a disgrace to the magazine. Christ, it's bad enough that you buy your suits at Klein's, but for God's sake, can't you get some that fit?"

"There's nothing wrong with my suits."

"Nothing that a can of kerosene and a match wouldn't fix. Give me one afternoon, okay? We'll have you looking human."

"Lou, I'm not a dandy. Never will be."

"Looking like a grownup human being don't mean being a dandy. Damn it, you represent the magazine out there on the streets. You can't do it looking like a wino. Give me one afternoon and I'll fix you up."

"Some day."

Marsczyk shook his head disgustedly and poured himself another drink. "What you got on Hobson so far?"

"You're giving me the story?"

"Of course, I'm giving you the story. You were there, you got a leg up."

"Well, as far as the shooter goes, we're either dealing with a criminal genius or an idiot," Taylor said. "Assuming, that is, Brownie was the target."

"What do you mean?"

"Two guys in the crowd get into a beef, one pulls out a gun and starts shooting, Brownie's in the way." Taylor took a sip of his drink. "It's a possibility, isn't it?"

The scotch was raw. Marsczyk didn't believe in buying the good stuff. It wasn't as though he couldn't afford quality. He had just installed a brand new GE television set, with a ten inch screen and a plastic case the manufacturer claimed was made of some miracle material they called Bakelite. He put it in his office so he wouldn't have to go home at night to catch the fights. The set resembled a space ship out of the Buck Rogers comic strip, with the swept back case that looked like the wings of a rocket. GE called it the Locomotive and Taylor knew they charged a mint for it.

Even though he hadn't done any actual copy editing in a decade or so, Marsczyk still wore his visor. He'd come up through Chicago's newspaper wars in the twenties and thirties when a dozen or so dailies had battled it out for readers while gangsters battled it out in the streets and he'd made his name by battling the gangs in his pages. Once a bomb had blown up his office, but he hadn't even slowed down; he'd staggered out into the newsroom, wiping the plaster dust from his clothes, sat down at a typewriter and typed up the story of the bombing.

Even though he now had just about the cushiest job in town, in his mind he was still the hard-punching city editor and when it became necessary, he could shrug off the slough that generally engulfed him and get the job done. He was hell to work for but Taylor recognized no reporter could help but respect him. Capote ought to work for Lou Marsczyk a while, he thought. The odd little kid would either turn into a reporter or go running back to Alabama.

"What do you say you go out and find out what happened?"

"Lou, are you sure? A third rate dancer gets popped. The man's on the bottom rung of show business. He's just barely got a foot on the show biz ladder. People would be more interested if the guy who runs the Flea Market on Times Square got it."

"Wrong. Brownie Hobson was a well-known figure in the show business world who was right on the verge of stardom when he was struck down by an assassin. Who knows why? Maybe something he saw while working in mob-owned night clubs, maybe because of some dark secret in his past." He lifted his drink, sighted over it as though it were a pistol and said, "Christ, Damon, you know the story."

"Lou, I don't think he's worth pumping up."

"Hobson knew a lot of people and some of them weren't exactly prime citizens. We don't know that some of them aren't tied up in this. How many times do I have to tell you? Don't prejudge a story. Get out in the streets and find out if there's anything to it or not. Go check this one out, see what you come up with."

"I'm telling you, Lou, there's nothing there."

"You don't seem to be able to remember the important things, Taylor. Let me just one more time give you Marsczyk's Law: whatever you're dealing with, there's always more to it then there seems. Always. I don't care what the story is, it's more complicated than it looks."

Taylor could have recited the law for him. He knew it by heart, having heard his editor say it at least three times a week since he'd joined the mag.

Marsczyk tossed off his drink, a signal that they were done. "If there's nothing there, we do a little profile. If there's anything to it, we run with it. Either way, it's a story. Get lucky, it might be a big one."

Horace McCall worked out of the central headquarters on Grand Street, so he drank just down the street in Irish Jack's, right next to Frank Lava's gunsmith shop. When Taylor called him, he suggested they meet there.

"You still got that fat expense account, ain't you?" McCall said.

"Yeah."

"Drinks are on you."

"They always are, aren't they?"

"Now don't be bitter, son." He hung up.

His bus got caught up in the lower Broadway traffic, so it took Taylor twenty minutes to reach Irish Jack's. McCall sat at the end of the bar, with a half empty whiskey glass in front of him. Irish Jack's was a working man's place that, because of its proximity to the station, had become a cop's bar. It didn't pretend to be anything else. Its clientele was made up of cops and neighborhood drunks. Anyone else who drifted in here would have quickly detected the place's atmosphere, become uncomfortable and left after a single drink.

Through the window, Taylor could see the clock in front of the beauty shop across the street. It said three-thirty in the afternoon but inside Irish Jack's, it might as well have been three-thirty in the morning. About a dozen booze hounds were hard at it. One man was passed out in a booth, his right cheek resting on the tabletop. Everyone ignored him. Half a dozen cops coming off the day shift were winding down at the bar, but the rest of the men there were wornout hard-time drunks. Down the bar, a fat red nosed guy in a flannel shirt tried to still his shaking hand as he raised his drink. McCall glanced at him, frowned and polished off his own drink. He tapped the empty glass on the bar and the bartender strolled over.

"One more," McCall said. "Taylor?"

"Jameson's on the rocks."

In a place like this, you ordered by brand and hoped that what they brought you was really what the label on the bottle said. He felt lucky; the Jameson's actually turned out to be Jameson's.

"So you want to know about the Hobson thing, huh?"

"Yeah. What have you got?" Taylor placed an envelope on the bar between them. "By the way, I bought you a new tie."

McCall slid the envelope into his jacket pocket without looking at it. "I can always use a tie." He reached into his brief case and pulled out a manila folder and handed it to Taylor. "The report, witness statements, everything we got. It ain't much."

"What's it add up to?"

"One thing that might tickle your toes. Two shooters."

"Two?"

"He had .32 and .38 slugs in him."

"One guy with two guns?"

"Fat fucking chance. No, there was two of them."

He wiped the sweat off of his glass. "Maybe two guys in the crowd get into a fight, shoot it out with each other and Brownie gets in the way?"

"No angles of entry. He was hit straight on five times. Brownie was the target, all right." He sipped his drink. "Two .38's, three .32's. All dead on. Had to be the target. How 'bout a sandwich?"

The food table in the back had a couple of loaves of bread, a jar of mustard and a warm roast on it. McCall sliced himself about half a pound of beef, slapped the meat onto a hunk of bread, laced it with mustard and covered it with another hunk of bread so that the sandwich stood two inches high.

"Nothing for you?"

"Not right now."

He looked at Taylor as if he thought the man a fool for passing up free food, no matter how bad it was. "Your choice."

He took a bite as they walked back to the bar. The man in the flannel shirt was reaching for McCall's drink.

"You touch that, I'll break your arm." McCall said. His voice was soft, which somehow made it more threatening.

The man scurried out of the bar. McCall called out to the bartender, "Did that son of a bitch touch these drinks?"

"I didn't see him." The bartender shook his head. "They're okay."

"Replace 'em." McCall said. "On the house."

For a moment, the bartender looked as if he was going to argue but he changed his mind and brought a new round. "Sorry about that bum," he said.

McCall raised his glass in salute. "Don't worry about it." Turning to Taylor, he said, "Let me sum this damn case up for you. A couple of guys went to the Savoy with the definite intent of putting Brownie Hobson away. Maybe a dozen people noticed them because they came in right before the floor show, shoved their way to the front and even threatened a guy who complained when they pushed his girl out of their way. As soon as Brownie came out, they popped him and ran for the door. Everybody else panicked and ran and the shooters were probably back downtown before we ever got there." He pointed to the folder. "You got all the details in there. Everything I got, you got."

"Thanks."

"You know how you can thank me?"

"How's that?"

"Bring me a couple of killers."

"That's not what I do, McCall. I just write about them."

He stared into his drink. "Not what you do, huh?"

"Nope."

"Then what the hell good are you?"

4

When he got home, Taylor spread the contents of the folder Mc-Call had given him on the kitchen table. Before starting in on it, he turned on the radio. On "Make-Believe Ballroom," Martin Block was introducing a Paul Whiteman record, so Taylor went up the dial to another station, looking for some blues. Whiteman was to music what Kathleen Winsor was to writing novels. Too old-fashioned, too sweet. It was like listening to syrup pouring out of a bottle. He found a rhythm and blues station just in time to hear the DJ do a jive talk introduction for Wynonie Harris's record of "Good Rockin' Tonight."

Much better.

He wasn't anxious to get to the file. It was just another chore, one that rarely paid off and probably wouldn't this time. He poured himself a glass of Jameson's. Since he'd gotten back from the war, he'd been feeling vaguely dissatisfied—with his work, his life, what have you. Nothing made a lot of sense anymore. Jameson's made a little sense but nothing else did.

He wondered when he'd started thinking of everything in terms of before and after the war, as though there were a clean-cut dividing line. Before the war, he'd loved his work, felt as if he were doing something important, something that made a difference. Now, though, he was going through the motions, writing crap for people who moved their lips while they read, people who got impatient and moved on to the next article if the blood didn't flow heavily enough on the page.

Maybe it was that simple. Maybe he just wanted to get back the feeling he used to have; maybe he wanted to feel he was making a difference. That was going to be impossible, though, because since the war, nothing mattered. The bomb they'd dropped on Hiroshima changed it all. Once you reached a point where all the life on the planet could go up at one time, who could get excited about a magazine story about a shooting in a dance hall?

Through the window, he could hear all the normal street sounds—the kids playing stickball, the rising noise level of conversations, guys calling out greetings as they came home from work, the traffic, all of the ordinary noises that made a block into a neighborhood. He'd grown up hearing these sounds. All of his life, from the time he was a little kid living on the Lower East Side, he'd loved this noise; it had been the soundtrack of his life, the lullaby that relaxed him for sleep, but then came the war.

Once he'd been drafted, he'd discovered how insulated life in the city had been. As a civilian, he'd always thought of himself as a citizen of the most sophisticated city in the world so he had to be one of the most sophisticated people. It didn't matter that he'd been around during the depression, he'd grown up feeling the optimism in the city's air, taking in the mood that everything was marching along toward the perfection promised by the 1939 World's Fair. Without ever thinking about it, he had shared that optimism. After the government declared him fit for duty and thrust him into boot camp, though, his thinking changed.

When he got to know the other recruits, Taylor discovered he was as petty, close-minded and insulated as any backwoods Mississippi farm kid. In fact, those farmers were better off than he was; at least they could do things with their hands—they could build or repair things. All he could do was pound out words on a typewriter.

In 1943, they sent him to Italy as a foot soldier, a grunt, part of the invasion force that landed on Anzio in January and he lay there, pinned down on the sand till May, trying to keep his ass alive while he watched his buddies die. On that beach, he discovered the world wasn't moving inexorably toward perfection after all. One morning, he was passing a cigarette to a guy in the next foxhole when a shell exploded and Taylor watched the arm that had reached out for a smoke go sailing through the air like a baseball bat that had slid out of a batter's hands at the end of a hard cut at a curve ball. That was the moment he'd discovered he was in hell.

Finally, in May, a heavy offensive rescued them and what was left of all the guys he'd landed with moved slowly inland, fighting their way step by step, day by day, to Rome. Once they secured Rome, most of the troops moved on to France while he was one of a handful left in Italy as a holding force, charged with keeping the Germans diverted from the main theater of the war in Normandy.

They were bait, targets. Their job was to make the Germans think there were a lot more of them than there really were, so they threw themselves at overwhelming forces damn near every day. Morning after morning, Taylor walked into the face of death and watched helplessly as most of his friends failed to walk back out. After Normandy, the idiots who made decisions moved the survivors into Germany, where he spent the rest of his war fighting his way to Berlin.

By the time they got there, he was no longer the guy who'd gone to the war. He'd seen too much. He'd also done too much, but that was another story, one he didn't tell himself very often.

Time to get to work. When he began thinking the way he was now, it was definitely time to get moving on a story. The second floor apartment was almost too hot to work in. In the summer time, especially summers as hot as this one shaped up to be, you could feel the temperature rise as you climbed the steps. After opening his shirt, Taylor turned on the fan and sat down with the pages. He'd read a couple of entries when the knock came at the door. When he opened it, Adolph Hitler was standing in the hall.

"How you doing?" Taylor said. "Come on in, have a drink."

"Love one," Hitler said.

As Hitler walked in, his boots clattered on the wooden floor. In the center of the living room, he paused, twirled like a model and said, "So what do you think?"

"Beautiful."

"How do you like the uniform?"

"Nice. You look great, just as threatening and maniacal as a lunatic should."

The only problem was that his hair was a little longer than you'd expect. He was Hitler who hadn't gone near a barber in months.

"I put it together out of old costumes I had around. Took a little doing, I'll tell you. Christ, you ever tried to put together a Nazi uniform without leaving the house?"

"I can truly say I haven't."

"It's a bitch, I can tell you that."

The windows were open and the fan wasn't helping much. It just circulated the hot air more freely. The street noises and the shouts of playing kids still floated through the window. You couldn't call them a distraction, though, because the noises were always there. After a while, they blended into the general background, became part of the city environment, like the opera singer who practiced every morning at three a.m.

"How long did the makeup take?"

"All afternoon. Finding the right skin tone wasn't easy. I had to blend it myself."

Hitler was actually Bob O'Bradovich, Taylor's downstairs neighbor. He was an actor who was obsessed with makeup effects and costuming. All his spare time—and since he was an actor, he had plenty of spare time—went into creating characters, mostly from history but occasionally from science fiction and horror. Whenever his knock came at the door, Taylor never knew if Abraham Lincoln, Babe Ruth or Sitting Bull was going to be standing in the hall. Once he came home to find the Frankenstein monster lurking outside his door. Linda, who lived upstairs, thought he was insane, so O'Bradovich avoided her door and came to Taylor's instead.

Taylor poured them each a shot of Jameson's and popped in a couple of ice cubes.

"Thanks," O'Bradovich said. He sat down at the kitchen table. Noticing the open folder, he said, "Working?"

"I'm looking into the Brownie Hobson thing."

"The dancer?" He indicated the radio with a jerk of his head. "Heard about it this morning. Radio's treating it like a big thing."

"Yeah, he was sort of close to being well-known and got himself shot on the dance floor of the Savoy in front of a thousand people. It's got all the ingredients. At least my editor thinks it does."

"That why *Crime Scene*'s on the story?"

"It might sell a few extra copies on the stands."

"You don't sound too enthusiastic about it."

"I'm not. It's…"

A commercial came on the radio for a furniture store. O'Bradovich signaled for silence and leaned forward to listen, mouthing the words as the announcer spoke them. When it was done, he frowned.

"I read for that job," he said. "Would have been a good payday. It's transcribed, the disc's playing on a dozen stations."

"Too bad you didn't get it," Taylor said.

"I could've done a better job. Did you hear that guy?" He shook his head. "He's about as convincing as Brett Morrison is playing the Shadow."

"You don't like Morrison?"

Taylor sighed inwardly. At one time, he'd hung out in reporter's bars, arguing about Aristotle, about books—once before the war, he'd spent an entire drunken evening with a couple of other writers debating whether Ben Hecht was going to advance the art of the novel or whether his movie work was going to ruin him forever. Now he talked about who made the best Shadow on the radio. And he didn't even give a damn about that; he spoke just to allow O'Bradovich a chance to answer.

The answer didn't make any difference anyway. He'd been around this town long enough to know that no actor ever fully approved of the work of any other actor and always had something bad to say about anybody else's performance.

"You ever hear Orson Welles when he was doing that show?"

Taylor shook his head. "I'm not a big listener."

"Orson, now, he was the Shadow. Show's been going downhill since he left."

"Didn't you work with Welles?" Since he knew what was coming, he said it as a prompt.

"I did a bunch of Mercury Theaters for him. Greatest damn working experience I've ever had. You know he never rehearses?"

"That a fact?"

"Yep. We used to do a read through for time, another one for sound effects and Orson wouldn't show up at either of them. Then he'd come in and do the show. He wanted the lines to sound as if he'd never said them before."

"So he never said them before?"

"Right. It worked for him, but me, Christ, I'd be terrified." He finished off his drink. "Just between us, Damon, I could name you a couple of times he'd have been better off if he had rehearsed."

Taylor wiped the sweat from his forehead with a dish towel. "Well, still, sorry about the commercial."

O'Bradovich reached across the table, drew the bottle over and poured himself another drink. "That's the game," he said. "Lose more than you win. I'm still up for the Miller play, though."

"The Miller play?"

"Thing called *Death of a Salesman*. It's by a guy named Arthur Miller."

"Never heard of him."

After adding a couple of cubes from the ice bucket, he swirled the whiskey in his glass, looking at it as though the color fascinated him.

"He had a play on Broadway a couple of years ago. A disaster. Only ran four performances. This one's ought to do better. It's a good script."

"You up for the salesman?"

"Naw, he's an old guy. Lee J. Cobb's already attached to that part. My part's Biff, the son. It's good, real meaty. I get to catch my old man in bed with another woman."

"Hope you get it."

"It's down to either me or Arthur Kennedy. Kennedy's okay but he's too Hollywood. Looks like I'm a lock." He sipped his drink. "So, what's the story with the dancer?"

Outside, the stickball kids were arguing over whether a player was safe or out at home. It sounded as if a fight was about to break out. Taylor walked over and glanced out the window. Home plate was in the middle of West 93rd Street, right in front of his stoop. Tommy Reiser, who lived in the basement apartment of his brownstone, saw Taylor and waved.

He waved back, satisfied that the hassle wouldn't get beyond the yelling stage. "Don't know what the story is yet. You had dinner?"

"Not yet."

"Too hot to cook. Get changed. We'll hit a restaurant."

"Want to go down to Lindy's?"

"I've got to work tonight. Let's stay in the neighborhood."

"How 'bout the automat?"

"I said a restaurant."

"Bobby Carlisle's, then. Give me twenty minutes."

He tossed off his drink and went back upstairs to change. Taylor picked up the file again, knowing he had time to read a few pages; it was going to take O'Bradovich more than any twenty minutes to get out of that makeup.

The heat assaulted them the moment they walked out the front door onto the stoop. "Jesus," O'Bradovich said, "it's like being hit in the head by a hammer, isn't it?" They walked slowly over to Broadway and down to Bobby Carlisle's steakhouse. O'Bradovich sighed with relief when they walked in. It was a refrigerator inside the restaurant. The air conditioner was turned up as high as it could go. From their table, they could see out onto Broadway, so they watched the foot traffic while waiting for their food.

People on the street moved slowly, conserving energy. Most of the men had taken off their suit jackets, carrying them draped over their arms. Every once in a while, though, a red-faced stubborn guy would walk by wearing his coat buttoned, as though this were some kind of brisk fall day.

After they'd polished off the steaks, O'Bradovich said, "You never told me, what's the story on the dancer?"

Out at Ebbets Field, the Dodgers were taking on Chicago in a night game and Taylor had figured on listening to the game while he went over McCall's file. That would fill the time until it got late enough to hit the streets. Still, they lingered over coffee, neither of them anxious to go back out into the heat.

"Be perfectly honest about it, I got no idea. All I can tell you is somebody didn't like him."

"I don't see you going to press on that."

"Nope. You know how it works, though."

"How's that?"

"What's going to happen is I'll start with a bio, go back over the guy's life as best I can, make it sound like something big time. Drop a few hints that it's all bigger than it really is. That's pretty much the boilerplate story."

"Not much to it, is there?"

"No, but it'll buy me some time."

"Time? Time for what?"

"Whatever got him killed came out of where he's been, what he did, who he talked to. I need to hit the streets, check it all out, talk to the people who knew him, hope something surfaces."

"You'll come up with a suspect that way?"

Without makeup or costumes, O'Bradovich looked nondescript, as though his inner power required a false nose to emerge. If you expected an actor to be striking looking, unusual in some way, you'd never peg O'Bradovich for a performer. In the past, though, he'd dragged Taylor to plays he'd been in and he'd been impressive. Taylor also listened to his neighbor's radio gigs and as an actor, he was convincing, even in junk.

Still, you expected an actor to be on, to be exuberant. Most of the ones Taylor knew bordered on obnoxious and looked for ways to go over the edge. They were always breaking into song or asking Taylor what he thought of them. O'Bradovich wasn't like that. He was too unassuming to draw a crowd—until he made himself up. Let him give himself a different face and he gained strength.

"I don't know if it's going to turn up a suspect, that's a little too much to hope for, but it might suggest a few possibilities. Not suspects, you understand, but possibilities. I'll do the overview for next week's issue and if the story generates any new leads, I'll follow up."

"And if there's no interest?"

"I'll have another story. There's always more crime."

The file didn't tell him a whole lot. Hobson had been shot by two different guns which belonged to two different guys who, according to the eye witnesses, were little tiny men who happened to be great big men. They were fat and skinny, blonde and black haired and wore suits and dance costumes. The testimony of every witness canceled out the description another one had given. Everybody had seen them but no two people had seen the same thing.

Hobson's police record was included. It was a hell of a lot more extensive than Taylor had thought it would be. Brownie'd dealt in stolen goods a time or two and had done a short stretch upstate. While he was still on parole, he developed a need to feel his fists pounding into people's heads. He got picked up for assault entirely too many times and wound up getting sent back for assault with intent. When he got out this time, though, he found a way to beat people up legally. He became a bouncer and had stayed clean for the past half dozen years or so—as clean as a guy who worked in clubs could stay, that is. He knew a bunch of bad guys but that was part of the job description.

When the game ended— the Dodgers won—Taylor checked his watch. Ten-thirty. Late enough to go see the man who knew all about everybody who worked in night clubs, the man who could tell you everything about everyone, especially if they wanted to keep it hidden.

5

Taylor passed under the canopy of the Stork Club and through the revolving door into the club. Men and women in evening clothes packed the anteroom, trying to look nonchalant and sophisticated as they passed bribes to the headwaiter, trying to get him to open the chain that barred their entrance to the main room. Taylor made his way past them, ignoring the scowl he got from a woman in her forties who wore more makeup than O'Bradovich used to create the Elf King.

When he reached the maître d's station, Sherman Billingsley flashed him a smile and strolled casually over. Billingsley was a dapper man who looked impeccable in his tuxedo and who seemed to believe that a good fashion sense could overcome his lack of height.

"Damon, you've been away too long."

"How are you, Sherman?"

"Fine, fine." Billingsley couldn't help but quickly take in Taylor's suit. He was too polished to let his disapproval show on his face. "You'll have a table up front?"

"No, I'm just here to see the man."

"Are you on his list?"

"I guess. I know I used to be."

He checked a list they kept at the entry station. When he found Taylor's name, he nodded approvingly and said. "I'll show you to his table."

"I know where it is."

"Of course you do. Indulge me. Let me escort you. It's good for people to see me with members of the press."

"Even if nobody knows who I am?"

"Damon, Damon, everybody knows you. You're a legend. Like Runyon himself." He let go of his studied formality, letting a little of the Brooklyn in his soul shine through.

The dance floor was crowded. A couple of dozen couples turned and twirled to a tune by Guy Lombardo, who nodded and smiled from the bandstand like a duke greeting the serfs. He jerked his baton up and down mechanically, looking as though only his arm motions were keeping him awake. The dancers looked like robots. They were much more restrained than the ones uptown at the Savoy. These people looked like they were trying out the steps they'd learned at Arthur Murray's studios. Taylor figured a sizable number of them had black footsteps placed on the kitchen floor linoleum at home to use as guides when they practiced. Lombardo's band, though, deserved this sort of audience. When he heard them play, Taylor always wanted to check to make sure the musicians were awake.

Walter Winchell was so much at home at his table that he might as well have been in his own apartment. He used the Stork Club as his office, so he was at this table every night. Around ten each evening, he came here and, over a never-ending bottle of champagne, held court over the steady stream of flacks and minor league celebrities who dropped by to flatter him unmercifully, treating him as if he really were as important as he thought he was. The flacks hoped the treatment would be enough to get him to run their items in his daily gossip column, which he put together—Taylor would never say he wrote it because that would imply that it was written—here in the club. The Broadway babes and second rate show biz big shots just wanted their names mentioned.

Taylor walked over to his table and stood across from him, watching the public relations guys, the managers and agents all fighting for his attention, while he pretended not to see or hear them. When he noticed Taylor, he pushed his hat back rakishly—he never took it off because he was sensitive about his baldness.

"Damon," he said, "sit down." He waved his hand dismissively toward the crowd around him. "These guys'll leave us alone."

The flacks scattered.

All reporters and sometimes, depending on his mood, Taylor, joined in hating Winchell because he was much more of an actor than a newsman. It was the one thing they had in common; liberals, conservatives, communists, the apolitical, the sports guys, society dames—all of them, no matter what their differences, joined together in their detestation of Winchell.

The man simply wasn't a newspaper guy. He'd come out of show business and had never drifted very far from it. He'd begun as a boy singer in a review called *School Daze*, the same show that had spawned Georgie Jessel and Eddie Cantor. In the bars at night, reporters still spoke wistfully, regretting the fact that, back when the show was running, nobody had placed a bomb in the theater and spared the world that trifecta.

After he grew too big to be a kid singer, Winchell did what everybody connected with show business did; he changed his name—he'd been born Weinschel. Then, instead of continuing to sing, he somehow stumbled onto a job as the gossip columnist for *The Vaudeville News*. When his column caught on, newspaper guys, especially the ones who could actually write, figured he must have made a deal with the devil. Winchell had a prose style that reminded you of a jackhammer tearing up a sidewalk. When Hearst hired him as a columnist and his success increased incredibly, growing to include radio, they were convinced that the selling of the soul story was true.

Now, Winchell worked out of the Stork Club, never going near the Hearst offices. Just a few weeks ago, Lou Marsczyk had given Taylor his theory on why Winchell never came near the city desk: "There's real reporters there. You think that silly bastard wants to walk past real reporters in a real newsroom? They'd mangle the son of a bitch, run him through the presses."

Of course, a lot of the resentment grew out of jealousy. Winchell had what every newspaper writer wanted: a huge, adoring following and an expense account the size of New Jersey. The whole city read his column daily and every Sunday night, 50,000,000 people across the country tuned in to hear him on the radio. Why, Taylor couldn't say. Winchell was as vacuous as a marshmallow and as melodramatic as a fire engine, rattling off his copy so fast that he seemed to feel that if he spoke slowly people would understand how stupid and simplistic most of the stuff he said really was. If you didn't give a damn who Orson Welles beat up in a Spanish nightclub that week, Winchell had nothing to tell you but he insisted on telling you anyway, speaking so quickly that he always appeared to be in danger of running out of items before the show ran out of time. He claimed to have been timed speaking 220 words a minute but Taylor thought that speaking that quickly and saying nothing was like operating a machine gun that fired garbage. He sprayed crap all over the place and left a stench behind. Winchell had never broken a story and wouldn't know how to go about it if he decided to.

What he did know was everybody in town.

As the mob scurried away, Taylor sat opposite him. Winchell signaled for his personal waiter, who appeared out of nowhere.

"Good to see you, Damon. What'll you have?" Winchell spoke as quickly in conversation as he did on the air.

"Jameson's on the rocks."

"And my usual," he said. As the waiter walked away, he said, "How've you been, son? Haven't seen you around lately."

"Been busy, Walter."

Winchell looked down at the table. It was covered with scraps of paper. Later on tonight, he would staple them together onto a sheet of newsprint, draw in ellipses for transitions and have his assistant run it over to the paper where his copy editor would make it look and sound like a column.

"I've seen your byline," he said. "You're doing good stuff over there at *Crime Scene*."

"Thanks."

He took a drink of his champagne. Looking into the glass and not at Taylor, he said, "I still miss him, you know," he said.

"Me, too."

"You and him, Damon, you two are about the only real friends I ever had."

Taylor was surprised that Winchell considered him a friend. He'd never treated him like one.

"You know," Winchell continued, "Runyon didn't really open up to very many people. It's like he knew everybody in town and not a damn soul knew him. You ever wonder why we were his friends?"

Whenever Taylor ran into Winchell, the older man brought up Damon Runyon, invoking the man's name as though preparing to pray, which made sense because he'd always adored Runyon as if he'd been God. The two of them had walked the same streets since the Twenties and had been buddies, a fact that came as a surprise to most people who read Damon Runyon's stories. Winchell appeared in them as "Waldo Winchester" and Runyon never missed an opportunity to make him look ridiculous.

Taylor always suspected that Runyon had been a little jealous of Winchell's success. Runyon may have been king of the city, but Winchell had a national following. Since he'd been on radio continuously since 1929, Winchell had built up the bigger name. It didn't matter that Runyon was the best crime reporter in the city and damn near the best sports columnist, or that his short stories had made him a very rich man. More than a dozen movies had been made from them or that right now, even though Runyon had been dead for close to two years, a Broadway show was being talked about, based on the two Nathan Detroit and Sky Masterson stories.

To Runyon, none of that had mattered. What counted was that in the country as a whole, Winchell was better known. That was the simple fact Runyon had never been able to get beyond. What had always driven him crazy was that out there in the sticks, Winchell wasn't considered an empty-headed clown, a second-rate entertainer, as he was here in town. People around the country who listened to his radio shows thought he was actually delivering news; they saw him as the dashing newsman with a press card in his hat—and one of the reasons real reporters laughed at Winchell was that he actually did wear a press card in his hat. He had even once demanded that the early edition be scrapped and page one remade to feature his latest scoop.

When you got right down to it, Winchell wasn't fit to sharpen Runyon's pencils. Even though Runyon tried really hard to give the impression that he had never put any effort into his stuff, that it just flowed as naturally as lemonade, he had worked his ass off at reporting all his life. "Son," he said to Taylor back in the old days, "News writing is the most important calling a man can aspire to." Occasionally, he shook his head in wonder and asked aloud how Winchell had stumbled into the newspaper business. "Christ," he said, "The idiot tripped over a career the way you would a brick in the street."

Still, they were friends and Winchell treasured his friendship. When Runyon died, Winchell went into a despair that he was just now beginning to come out of.

"You know," he said, "that last couple of years, when they'd torn out his throat because of the cancer and put in metal pipes so he could breathe and eat, I was the only friend he had left. You were away in the war and all his other friends," he spat the word, "wouldn't have a Goddamn thing to do with him anymore. The bastards turned their backs on him when he needed them the most." He waved a hand. "I'm not talking about you. I know you'd have stood by him if you hadn't been off fighting, but, Jesus Christ, I was the only one who was there to give him a hand. After everything he did for those people and this business, they treated him like a leper."

"I know."

Of course, Taylor knew. Winchell told him the story every time the two of them ran into each other. It was a ritual Winchell went through, a way of dealing with how badly he missed Damon Runyon. Tonight, Taylor did what he did every time Walter told the story: he listened as if he'd never heard it before.

"He wouldn't even go to Lindy's anymore and you know how important Lindy's was to him," Winchell said. "Took to hanging around here with me. He wouldn't talk. He had one of those tracheal tubes and some kind of device he could speak through, but he wouldn't use it. Said he'd be damned if he'd let anybody hear him squawking like a movie robot. He used to write notes. Still, as sick as he was, he never stopped being a reporter. I'd drive him all over the city so he could watch the cops at crime scenes. We were out there every night. Did you see the columns he wrote about those trips?"

When Taylor had gotten back from the war, one of the first things he'd done was to go down to the morgue at the *American* and read everything Runyon had written while he'd been overseas. He'd made copies of the best of it; they were bound in leather on his shelf at home, next to Runyon's books.

He lifted his glass. "To Damon."

"There'll never be a better man."

Winchell raised his champagne and tossed it off. His waiter immediately appeared and refilled his glass. That always bothered Taylor; he had trouble warming up to a man who couldn't be bothered to fill his own glass.

"You never just drop by, Damon," Winchell said. "What do you need? What can I do for you?"

"I'm working the Brownie Hobson story."

"Dancer? Got himself shot at the Savoy?"

"That's the one. What do you know about him?"

"I know nobody's going to miss him very much. He was one mean son of a bitch. If you're looking for suspects, just about everybody who ever met him will fill the bill."

"Why? What'd he do that was so bad?"

"I hear that when he was a kid, maybe thirteen, fourteen, he used to hang out on the corner with an umbrella. When a younger kid came by, Brownie'd trip him with the umbrella and when the kid hit the ground, he'd jump on him and beat the living hell out of him. Just because he thought it was funny."

Winchell watched a flack give a note to his waiter. Taylor recognized the public relations man; he'd been a reporter on the *American* before he'd been fired for being drunk on the job. The waiter raised his eyebrow and when Winchell nodded, he brought the note over. After he read it, Winchell crumpled it and dropped it in the ash tray. From about fifteen feet away, the flack watched the whole thing, his hopeful expression fading.

"Walter, if we all got judged by the stuff we did when we were thirteen..."

"I know, most of us outgrow it. Brownie never did. You know anybody else in town who became a bouncer because he liked to beat people up?"

"He did some time. Was he mobbed up?"

"If he was, I didn't hear about it. What I do hear is that he was muscle for hire. Even when the dance group got going, he'd still take the occasional muscle job. Did mob guys hire him once in a while? I can't say."

Winchell prided himself on his knowledge of the mob. He thought of himself as some sort of honorary FBI man and it infuriated him that J. Edgar Hoover was still denying there was any such thing as a mob. Winchell had even taken the credit for Louis Lepke's surrender, walking the mobster into J. Edgar's office, accompanied by a dozen photographers.

"Hobson was too unpredictable, you know?" Winchell said. "He didn't have the self-discipline to make a contribution to anybody's gang."

"Two guys popped him. They had enough balls to do it in a public place, standing right next to hundreds of people. I'm betting these were guys who knew what they were doing."

"You want me to ask around?" Winchell said. "See what I can come up with?"

"I'd be grateful."

"Consider it done. Let me ask you a question. It's something I always wondered, always wanted to ask you."

"What's that?"

"Most people couldn't get close to Runyon? How'd you do it?"

"Didn't I ever tell you that story?"

He shook his head. His waiter took that as a signal to pour more champagne.

"Getting close to him wasn't anything I planned. Fact is, he sought me out. When I first started at the *American*, he sent for me. Even then he didn't bother to come to the office very often. I met him at Lindy's. We talked a little, and he must have liked me. He said as long as I was going to be on the paper, he'd better help me out because if I did a lousy story, people might see my first name and think it was him. So, he showed me around, introduced me to people, sort of took me under his wing. For a couple of months, till he decided I didn't need it any more, he edited my copy. Let me tell you, it was the best damn crash course in reporting anybody ever got."

"Not to mention friendship."

"You got that right."

Winchell raised his glass again. "Damn, I wish he was here."

Sitting at his private table, surrounded by acolytes, fawning hacks looking to be used, he seemed lonely.

6

If you wanted a walking definition of the word "huge" all you had to do was point at Big Joe Turner. Not only was his body massive but his personality was enough to dwarf the Chrysler Building. Turner's laugh had enough energy to warm an apartment. Taylor heard that laugh a lot during the hour he interviewed Turner for the profile.

Now Big Joe Turner folded his hands across his waist and said, "Got everything you need?"

"For the profile, sure, but I want to ask you a few things about what happened the other night."

"The dancer that got his ass shot off, you mean?"

"Yeah."

"Tell you what, Sport, how 'bout you buy me breakfast?"

"Okay."

He was staying at the Hotel Holland, a theatrical hotel on Forty-Second Street, right around the corner from the Hotel Dixie. "And let me tell you," Big Joe said, "There ain't no way in hell you're going to catch me staying in a place called the Dixie. No, sir, by God."

They were in his room on the fourth floor. The sound of the horns of taxi cabs and the wheeze of buses floated through the open window.

"Saw that automat down the block," Turner said. "Food any good?"

"Serviceable. You don't mind walking a couple of blocks, we can go to the Stage Deli. Food's a lot better."

"I heard about that place. Show business people go there, right?" He mashed out his cigarette in an overfilled ash tray.

"Yeah. And a lot of ballplayers."

"Got that good Jewish food? That corned beef, pastrami?" His face brightened as he spoke, already anticipating the feast.

"Best in town."

"Lead the way, my man."

He stood up and put on a sport coat that was big enough to use as a tent for boy scouts. It struck Taylor as odd that Big Joe didn't seem to be aware of his size. It was as if in his mind he was no larger than anyone he passed on the street.

Just more talented. Big Joe had made a splash since he'd hit town. "Funny," he said, "First time I was here, with that spirituals show, nobody noticed me at all. This time it's a little different." His picture had appeared on the entertainment pages, the reviews of his show had been fabulous and he'd become this week's big thing. As they walked, he was aware of the recognition in the eyes that caught his and when a person came up and asked for an autograph or said hello, Big Joe was unvaryingly kind and responsive, signing his name in a scrawl as big as he was, taking time to learn the man's name and using it when he spoke to the guy. But he never stopped moving. He stepped forward steadily, purposively, like a fullback determined to pick up the first down his team needed to stay in the game.

When they walked into the deli, Max Asnas looked over from behind the counter. "Well, now," he said, "if it ain't Damon Taylor. Been a while, boy. Who's your giant friend?"

"Hello, Max. This is Big Joe Turner." Turning to Joe, he said, "Max and his brother own this place."

"We have that misfortune," Max agreed. "What can I get you?"

Checking out the slabs of lunch meat behind the counter, Big Joe turned to Taylor and grinned. "You on an expense account, ain't you?"

"That I am."

"What you say we see what kind of hole we can knock in it?"

After sausage and eggs, a pastrami sandwich, a corned beef sandwich and three slices of cheesecake the size of a record album, which he declared the best he ever had, Big Joe wiped his mouth with a napkin, lit up a Lucky Strike and said, "So, you got some more questions for me, you said?"

"Yeah. Where the hell do you put all that food?"

Max Asnar looked at Big Joe admiringly. "Have to tell you, Damon, I like this boy."

"You're the best, Max," Big Joe said.

Taylor said, "I'm looking into the Brownie Hobson shooting. You know of anything that can help me? Anything you saw or heard around the club?"

He waved a massive hand. "Cat from *Jazz Monthly* looking into a murder? What's wrong with you, Taylor? You don't want to go messing around with something like that."

"I'm just doing a free lance piece on you for *Jazz Monthly*. I work for *Crime Scene*."

"You're a crime reporter?"

"That's right."

"Then what the hell you doing writing about me?"

"I like your music."

He glanced down at Taylor in surprise. "How you know my music? White boy like you, what do you know about the blues?"

"I've been listening to the blues all my life, Joe." He told Turner about seeing him in the clubs in Los Angeles. He told him how fresh and exciting his music had sounded, how much he'd enjoyed it. He thought about telling him how, when he got back from the war, Big Joe's music was the only thing that made him feel alive, the only thing that generated any energy in him, but he figured that was a lot of baggage to unload on a man he barely knew.

"I'm trying to figure you going into some of the clubs I played out there, man. You know, some of them, white boys ain't the most welcome sights."

"I never had any trouble."

"That a fact?"

"Always been my theory that other people will pretty much treat you the way you treat them."

"Mine, too. Don't always work out that way, though. Maybe the brothers could see you dug the music and gave you a pass."

"Could be."

Big Joe checked his watch. From across the table, Taylor could see the glint of the diamonds encrusted in the face. "Think I got time for another beer. Mr. Max, one more?"

There was no way Max Asnar was going to deliver to a table. He'd once ordered Hank Greenberg out of the place because Greenberg insisted on having his food brought to his booth. Taylor walked over to the counter and brought back a couple of Blatz's. When he put one in front of Turner, the bluesman looked at it as though he didn't quite recognize it as beer and then grunted, "Thanks."

"Let me ask you about Brownie Hobson."

"Hell, man, I didn't pay no attention to that cat. He's a dancer, a specialty act, you know what I mean? He fills the time while I catch my breath."

"You guys were all backstage together, though, Joe."

"Man, I'm backstage, I ain't paying no attention to nobody else. Especially that guy. First time I seen him, he was acting like he was this big man, more important than anybody else on earth. Man, how could a guy that tiny, that trivial, have that big a sense of his own importance?"

"So you didn't pay any attention to him? None at all?"

"Come on, you seen me on stage, ain't you? You seen how hard I work." he said. "I get me a break between sets, all I want to do is wipe down the sweat, grab a quick drink, smoke a cigarette." As if to prove his point, he lit up another Lucky. "I don't want to be bothered by nobody. Especially nobody like Brownie Hobson. Hell, man," he waved his cigarette in the air, "that cat was about the most unpleasant dude I ever saw in a music club. He comes into the room, it gets downright frosty, you know what I mean?"

Taylor stopped writing and looked at him, encouraging him. "What'd he do to cause you to think he was so cold, Joe?"

"First night I seen him, he was slapping a girl."

"He was? What was going on?"

"Damned if I know. I was walking to my dressing room, I see him slap her, hard, man, and then he turns his back and goes into his dressing room. Leaving her standing there."

"Who was the woman?"

"I don't know. One of those backstage broads I'm guessing."

"Anything else you notice about him?"

"That same night, he's talking to one of the cats in that dumbass little dance troop of his. This cat's trying to tell him he needs more money, says he knows how the act's making more money now and he's the real star of the show and he wants himself some of that bread he's pulling in for the man. This Hobson cat's just laughing at him, tells him he's got a contract and he ain't going to get a penny more than his deal says he's entitled to. The little cat tells him it ain't good enough, that maybe he'll have to quit and start up his own group and Hobson acts like that's the funniest damn thing he ever heard. Says if he tries something like that, he'll sue his ass off. He just goes into his dressing room, slams the door in the boy's face and you can hear him in there laughing."

"That's all there was to it?"

"Well, now, I don't know that it means anything but the boy did yell at him. Hell, it was more like he yelled at the locked door. Said he was going to get his fat ass."

"He threatened him?"

"Can't say what it means, man. You know how it is, you get pissed at a guy, you say things. Most of the time, it don't mean a thing."

"Who was the boy? You hear his name?"

He shook his head. "He was a young cat, greasy little bastard. That's all I know. Hell, man, you shouldn't have any trouble finding out his name. There's only three other guys in the act."

He was right about how simple it was going to be to find a name. Sam Fortune, the stage manager at the Savoy, told Taylor the man he was looking for was called Frankie DeMarco and that he lived in a boarding house between Sixth and Seventh on West 44th Street. As he crossed Sixth Avenue, Taylor noticed once more the street sign that declared the name of the street to be Avenue of the Americas. Back when he'd been mayor, Fiorello La Guardia, in a fit of insanity, had renamed the street, but he was the only person who'd ever called it by the new name. To everybody in the city, it was and always would be Sixth Avenue.

DeMarco's landlady, a woman as round as a basketball, held her cigarette in front of her face like a shield and stared suspiciously at Taylor. When he asked for Frankie DeMarco, she rubbed the hand that didn't have a cigarette in it on her stained checkerboard apron and said, "You a friend of that bum?"

"Never met him."

"Owes you money, too, huh? Most likely you can find him up at the corner, drinking away his rent money in O'Neal's."

"Thanks," Taylor said.

"You see him, you tell him he ain't got no money for me, he might as well not even come back here 'cause there ain't no way in hell he's getting in his room."

"Behind in his rent?"

"Hell, mister, he ain't paid since they invented money."

DeMarco stood at the bar, waving his arms to emphasize the story he was telling a couple of his drinking buddies. He was about as tall as a bottle of glue. His two friends towered over him, one on each side; DeMarco looked like a child standing between a couple of statues in the park. He broke out laughing at his own story and when he saw Taylor walk over, he ignored him, as though the reporter wasn't worth his time. The tale he was telling was about a seduction and to hear him tell it, he was the greatest lover since Casanova. Taylor waited a minute or so, but DeMarco just kept on, determined to pretend he wasn't there.

"DeMarco?" Taylor said. "Frankie DeMarco?"

He held his hand out like a traffic cop signaling a stop and kept on talking.

"You DeMarco?" Taylor said again.

He shoved his hand out again, making motions to push Taylor away. Reaching out, Taylor gripped his fingers and bent them backwards. DeMarco screamed and when Taylor continued to bend the fingers, fell to his knees.

"Jesus, Mister," he said.

His two friends acted as if they intended to get into it. One of them doubled up his fists, but when Taylor shook his head and said, "You don't really want to do that. You want to question whether he's worth what I'll do to you," the man unclenched them. Both of them walked away.

"We need to talk, DeMarco."

"Okay, okay. Just let go of my hand. Jesus, mister, you don't have to break my hand."

"What you say we get a booth?" Taylor said.

O'Neal's was a neighborhood bar with a decor that seemed to have been done by a person whose whole decorating idea was to keep the whiskey flowing. It was set up to pump out booze: a bar with lots of standing room took up the back of the room, a handful of scattered tables sat in front of it and there were a few booths over on the side. The floor looked as though the last time it had been swept was just before Pearl Harbor. Two of the tables, although no one sat at them, still had glasses and beer bottles on them. The jukebox had an out of order sign on it.

When they were seated in a booth, Taylor said, "My name's Damon Taylor. I'm a reporter for *Crime Scene*."

"You're a Goddamn reporter and you hurt me like that?" he whined, rubbing his hand. "What the hell's wrong with you? You didn't have to hurt me."

"Here's your lesson in common courtesy, DeMarco: when a person's trying to get your attention, you do not ignore him and when someone speaks to you, you acknowledge him. It's as simple as that."

"You break my damn fingers to give me a fucking lesson in good manners?"

I signaled the bartender. "What are you drinking?"

"You buying?"

"Sure."

"Single malt scotch."

Taylor shook his head sadly. "There's just no getting through to you, is there?" Taylor ordered them each a shot of Jameson's.

"That's good, too," DeMarco said.

"I hear you had a beef with Brownie Hobson the other night," Taylor said.

"That what this is about?" He looked surprised. "Brownie's shooting?"

"That's right."

His disappointment showed in his face and Taylor realized the dancer had somehow made up his mind that this was his big moment, that Taylor had cracked his fingers in order to do a story on him. Show people, he thought; they all believed that they were the story. Even a third rate club dancer convinced himself he was more important than a murder.

"I don't know nothing about Brownie getting popped," he said.

"You were there."

"Sure, but I was dancing, man. I get to doing my moves on the floor, I don't see nothing but music."

"Tell me about the fight."

"What fight's that?"

The bartender brought the whiskey. The single ice cube in the glass had almost melted away. Taylor asked for a glass of ice cubes and the bartender looked annoyed.

"The fight I've got in mind is the one you had with Brownie backstage a few nights ago. The way I hear it, you were demanding more money and he laughed in your face, humiliated you in front of everybody there."

"Oh, that fight."

"That's the one. How come you shot him?" You always threw an accusation around, if only to throw the man off-balance.

"Are you crazy? I didn't shoot anybody. Hell, man, I was right there dancing. How the hell could I have shot him?"

"Come on, DeMarco, get real. In this town, you can find a dozen people on the streets that'll pop him for fifty dollars."

"I swear to God, man, I didn't have anything to do with it. I didn't do nothing."

"Then who did?"

"Hell, man, how should I know?"

Taylor felt as though he were wallowing in garbage. It wasn't the bar that made him feel that way, even though it was a step or two below the ones he usually drank at; it was DeMarco. Being with him was like sitting at a table with a weasel.

"Look, Mr...." DeMarco said.

"Taylor. Damon Taylor."

"Look, Taylor, me and Brownie, hell, we went round and round all the time. Didn't mean a thing."

"I understand. So you didn't really want more money?"

"What?" He blinked four or five times, really fast, in confusion.

"What I hear is you demanded more money."

He twisted up in his seat, clutching his hands together as if he were looking forward to counting a bag of gold. "You know how it is, Taylor, you always want more money. Didn't you ever ask your boss for a raise?"

"Sure. I can't recall threatening him when he turned me down, though."

"Threatening? Christ, man, I never threatened anybody."

"I got witnesses say you did. I believe what you said was you were going to get his fat ass."

He tried a smile. It made him look feral. "I wouldn't call that a threat."

"Who shot him?"

"I got no idea."

"Let's try this: you argued with Brownie. He humiliated you, wouldn't give you a raise, so you hired a couple of guys to pop him. I'm betting you figure with Brownie gone, you'll take over the Lindy Hoppers and write yourself some checks the size of the ones Brownie was cashing."

"Man, you're crazy. You're so far out of it, you ain't even on this planet anymore."

"You got no intention of taking over the group?"

"Well, sure, I want to do that. I'd be a fool not to. Work it right, it's a money machine. I could do a hell of a lot more with it than Brownie ever did. But, Jesus, mister, I didn't have anything to do with shooting Brownie."

"Who shot him, DeMarco?"

"Damn it, I told you I don't know. Will you stop asking me that?"

"You got your rent money?"

"Huh?" He wasn't really good at keeping up with changes in the subject.

"I asked if you got your rent money. Your landlady said if you can't pay what you owe, don't bother to come back."

"That bitch. All I did for her, you'd think she'd give a guy a break." He looked at Taylor hopefully. "Hey, listen, I get a check in a couple of days. Can you lend me ten till then?"

7

The scheme was so simple that he was almost embarrassed to have come up with it. Guys getting ready for a job made all these elaborate plans, working everything out to the last detail, trying to cover every possibility, trying to work up other ways of looking at things in case something unexpected came up. The fact was that none of that was necessary.

All you needed was a little nerve.

And he had that. In spades. All of his life, if he'd been known for anything, it was his nerve. When he was a kid, people on the block had admired him because he'd never turn down a dare. Challenge him to do something and, by God, he'd do it.

"Hey, Mickey," a grown up would say, "See that car stopped for the light over there? Bet you won't run out in the street and jump in front of it when it starts moving."

"I'll do it for a nickel."

"You wouldn't dare."

So he jumped out in front of an oncoming Ford and stood stock still, hands on his hips, glaring at the driver, laughing at the panic in the man's eyes as he swerved, almost running up on the sidewalk to keep from hitting him. When the car passed, he swaggered over to the man who'd dared him.

"Give me my damn nickel," he said.

Oh, yeah, they respected his courage and it didn't take long for him to make the men on the block fear him and, you know, he enjoyed that feeling even more. When he was around ten, Mickey Arrelano—by now, people called him Crazy Mickey—joined up with some of the older kids who called themselves the Fourth Street Gang. Running with them, he discovered that he was good with his fists and feet and was especially good with a baseball bat. By the time he was around thirteen, he was carrying a gun and discovered that when the need popped up, he was pretty good with it, too.

It didn't take long for him to outgrow the Fourth Street Gang— he was too smart to mess around with those dummies. Since he was a little guy who didn't look very intimidating, he teamed up with a giant, Johnny Lee Schappelli, and the two of them started their own business. Mostly, they did enforcement work for the big boys. They'd make sure the bars bought the right beer and that the bordellos paid off on time, stuff like that, but when they weren't busy with that stuff, they followed their own interests—burglaries, the occasional robbery, small scale drug dealing, all that.

Last year, though, Johnny Lee had gone down; he'd always been impulsive and just a little bit too dumb to be going out by himself. He'd boosted the wrong guy. A stupid, senseless stickup. The mark had reached for his billfold, fear shining in his face like a lantern but came out with an army souvenir .45 instead and blew Johnny Lee to pieces. So now Mickey was working alone.

Even though he missed Johnny Lee, as far as work went, his partner's absence didn't make any difference. If you were clever enough, brave enough and mean enough, you didn't really need a partner and he was all of those things. His size didn't matter anymore. So, here he was, standing at the corner of Sixth Avenue and 39th Street, right here in the heart of the Garment District. Clouds of steam hissed from the upper floors of the buildings around him as the pressing machines up there in the lofts ironed out freshly manufactured clothes. The steam was thick enough to make it look like the buildings were on fire. The air was moist from the condensation of the steam and every once in a while drops of water fell, as if it were spastically raining. Crazy Mickey didn't give a damn. He wouldn't be here long.

The truck he'd been waiting for made its way through the heavy traffic on 39th Street. Traffic was insane here. Cars and trucks would roll along for maybe fifteen feet, come to a complete halt and lean on their horns until they could crawl another few feet. While the truck was caught in a stop, he walked over, opened the door and climbed into the passenger's side. Casually, without making a big deal of it, he showed the driver his gun.

"If you want to live," he said, "just keep on driving. Head straight on over to Ninth Avenue."

"I ain't got no money," the driver said. He was a fat man in a sweat-stained tee-shirt, with a well-chewed cigar in the corner of his mouth. "I don't collect no money. All I do is drop off cloth goods."

"Ain't after your money," Mickey said. "Head over to Ninth Avenue."

"You're the man with the gun, you're the man gives the directions."

"Good thing to keep in mind."

"What I want you to understand," the driver kept his eyes straight ahead on the truck in front of them and said, "is I'm a guy doing a job. I got no interest in this truck or what's in it. You want it, it's yours. The only thing I'm interested in is getting out of this alive."

"You ain't nearly as dumb as you look," Mickey said. "Turn north on Ninth Avenue."

The city had decided that the elevated trains were more trouble than they were worth, so they were dismantling the Ninth Avenue El. They drove along beneath the towers that had supported the tracks which had recently been taken down. The huge concrete structures looked like monuments to some kind of urban gods.

"You want a cigar?" the driver asked.

"Sure. Why not?"

"They're in the glove compartment. Want to get me one, too?"

He dug two cigars out of the compartment, unwrapped the cellophane and passed one over to the driver, who spat the stub he'd been chewing out the window and replaced it with the new cigar. Within seconds, it was as chewed up and used looking as the stub it had replaced.

"There's matches in the glove box, too," he said.

Mickey lit his own cigar and passed the matches over to the driver. This was life the way it ought to be, he thought, just rolling along with a good cigar, a driver who knew the score and a truck full of stuff that was going to make a good impression on the man, which meant that in the long run, it was going to make Mickey a lot of money. Right now, Crazy Mickey Arrelano was one happy man.

So they called him Crazy? What was so crazy about big bags of money?

Still, he thought maybe he wouldn't let anybody use that name anymore. It didn't have any dignity to it.

The towers were covered with graffiti. As they drove, Mickey tried to read it, but reading was a slow process for him so he missed most of the words. When they got further uptown, the tracks hadn't been taken down yet and they drove under the rails. Since the tracks blocked the sun, it was cooler and darker beneath them.

The driver exhaled smoke and said, "Thing that's got me worried is you might think I'm a danger to you because I seen your face. I need to take a minute right here to tell you that ain't the case. I ain't a danger to you for no reason."

"I hear you."

"Like I said, it ain't my truck and the stuff in it ain't mine either. For all I know, and as a matter of fact this strikes me as the truth of the matter, you're the rightful owner of all of it and my rightful job is to deliver it straight to you and drive you wherever you want to go."

"I like the way you think. Just keep driving."

"Just tell me where to make the turns," the driver said.

At Cortland Street, he told the driver to stop.

"Look, mister," the driver said.

"Give me your driver's license," Mickey said.

The man handed it over. Mickey Arellano read it over slowly, his lips moving. Then he slid it into his pocket.

"Here's the deal," he said, raising the gun, reminding the driver of its threat, "If you figure still being alive is good enough for you and you don't feel any strong compulsion to tell the cops or anybody about how this thing went down, you can get out here and walk away alive. There's a subway stop right down there at the corner that'll get you back downtown. You can live. Or you can tell some-body about this and I'll come back and kill you. I got your address here on your license so you know I can find you any time I want to."

"Hey, mister, I don't know how many ways I can say it. I get paid whether this truck gets where it's going or not. You want it, you got yourself a truck."

"Get out and walk."

He drove the truck over to Brooklyn, parked it in a safe garage and then made a phone call. "Got something your boss might be inter-ested in," he told the man who answered the phone. "Coco Chanel truck and all the stuff in it."

"Why would we be interested in that?" The voice asked.

"I guess you don't know she's using non-union truckers?"

"I'll pass this on. Give me a phone number."

Mickey gave the man a number and smiled. The boss was bound

to be impressed with this one, which meant that he'd be impressed with Mickey, which meant good things and good times were just around the corner.

8

Taylor was coming up on deadline so he went back to the office and worked the phones for a couple of hours. The city room was the size of one of those furniture warehouse stores up in the Bronx and was crammed with desks, each with a telephone and a Smith-Corona on top of it. Water pipes ran across the ceiling and you could hear the steady hiss of water heating. Two dozen guys sat at their desks typing furiously, while half a dozen others, carrying cups of coffee, wandered through the room, stopping to kibitz with the guys who were writing.

Since Taylor was a contributing editor, his desk was in the corner nearest Lou Marsczyk's office. He had a window in front of the desk and as he called people, Taylor stared down at the pedestrians and the traffic five floors below. When he'd run out of people to call, he didn't know a thing he hadn't known before.

He cranked out the standard boilerplate story, emphasizing the anti-social aspects of Brownie's background, working hard to establish the idea that the dancer, if he wasn't mob-connected himself, hung around with people who were. He used the fact that the two shooters had worked calmly, professionally and efficiently to suggest that Hobson might have been professionally hit.

The story stank. Read it carefully and you'd have to conclude that the writer didn't know a damn thing. The piece was a hash of rumors, hints, educated guesses and implications. Still, he called for a copy boy and hoped the stench from the story would go away with the kid who carried it to the copy editor. Then he walked over to Dick's Bar and Grill, the reporter's bar down near the Brooklyn Bridge the guys from the office frequented, to wash away the frustration of not being able to nail the story.

Funny, these days he didn't give much of a damn about anything, but not being able to get the story bothered him. If your work was all you had, he thought, then even if it was sell-out work, you wanted to do it right.

Lou Marsczyk sat at the bar, nursing a glass of Scotch. Taylor sat down next to him and signaled for Dick to bring him a drink.

"How are you, Dick?" He said when the bartender arrived.

"I am being crucified." Dick waved a fist in the air, "They are crucifying me!"

Dick's mustache made him look like something out of a silent western. He held up a bottle of Jameson's for Taylor's approval. After Taylor gave it by flashing a circled thumb and index finger, Dick poured him a glass, put it on the bar and slid a bowl of peanuts over to him.

"The story stinks," Taylor said.

"Figured it would," Marsczyk said. "You establish beyond a doubt that he was dead?"

"That's about all I could do."

"It's a start. I take it you hinted at the mob stuff?"

Taylor nodded. "Only angle I had."

"Good enough. Where do you go next?"

"You want me to stay on it?"

"You're suggesting maybe you nailed it and it's time to move on?"

"Of course not. But is it worth staying on?"

Marsczyk finished off his drink and slid the glass to the far edge of the bar. Dick ambled casually down—he made everything look casual—and refilled it. He topped Taylor's off also, as though it were a draft beer or a cup of coffee.

"I ever tell you about Ed Rathbone?" Marsczyk said, his voice a soft drawl.

"Nope."

"I was a police reporter in Chicago, my first major beat. Ed Rathbone was a dentist on the west side, committed suicide in his office. I'm covering it. Routine as all hell, two graphs buried inside. Only reason he's making the paper at all is he's a precinct captain for the Democratic machine. So, I'm cranking out the boilerplate, but something doesn't smell right. To this damn day, I don't know what it is but something starts tugging at my brain. I spend a couple of days poking around, I find out some dental records are missing from his files. Turns out they belong to Frank Nitti." He turned on his stool, faced me and continued, using his drink as a pointer. "Nitti was one crazy son of a bitch, didn't want anybody to be able to identify him any way at all. It's like he thought maybe he'd take a bite out of a sandwich at a hit and the feds would see the sandwich and come after his ass."

Taylor never knew how seriously to take his stories. Once, though, he'd said something that was so far beyond belief that Taylor couldn't accept it. Marsczyk had claimed that a Mother Superior in Chicago had turned out to be a voodoo priestess and had converted the entire crew of nuns under her charge. They'd taken to sacrificing goats in the nunnery. The story had been so warped and loony that Taylor had felt compelled to check it out. It turned out to be true, which raised Marsczyk's credibility a notch or two. Since then, Taylor had tended to take the man's stories a little more seriously.

"I kept pushing, kept digging," Marsczyk said. "Everybody was happy with the suicide call. The cops, my editor, Nitti and his boys, didn't a damn soul want to turn over the first leaf, but I kept pushing it and pretty soon we turned the shooter, a low level mob guy who claimed he'd been working on his own, said it was nothing more than a robbery gone bad. He would have hung but damned if he didn't up and commit suicide while he was waiting for trial."

"Never tied it to Nitti?"

"You kidding? Nitti's like the last thread in a cable-knit sweater. You can't get near his ass. He didn't even like how close I got."

"He give you a hard time?"

"Couple of his boys knocked me around a little." He shrugged. "Part of the job, that's all. Nothing more than that."

"So you're suggesting maybe I haven't quite gotten to the bottom of this story?"

"The whole thing stinks."

"How so?"

"It's a hit designed to send a message." He ticked the factors off on his fingertips. "Two shooters when one would do. Different caliber pistols, just so we'll be sure there's two of them. Public place, where we got maybe 2500 possible witnesses, no finesse at all, just walk up and start pulling the trigger, might as well be wearing signs saying 'We don't give a shit who sees this, 'cause you'll be too fucking terrified to say a word.' No, they wanted it done in public, with a crowd around. Nobody else hurt, they got exactly who they went after and with all those people around, didn't hurt another soul. And they just stroll out."

"So the message is, we can do whatever the hell we want to."

"That's it. It doesn't matter how many people are around, how safe you think you are, none of that. We want you, we got you."

"Wonder who they're sending that message to?"

Lou Marsczyk stood. Digging in his pocket, he left a few bucks on the bar to cover the drinks. "See you, Dick," he called out.

Dick waved a hand in disgust from the other end of the bar. "Go away. Never come back. Go away."

"Who are they sending a message to?" Marsczyk repeated, stopping on his way to the door. "I don't know. What you say you go hit the streets, maybe find out?"

9

In the summertime, the people who lived on Forsyth Street down on the Lower East Side moved out onto the sidewalks. When it got hot, the women all gathered on the stoops on the shady side of the street, watching their kids play. The ones who got there early brought out lawn chairs and placed them in shady spots. Taylor found Janie Hobson sitting with a friend in the shade of the stairway that led up to the Second Avenue El. When he introduced himself, the friend, a blonde with a kerchief tied over her hair, stood up slowly, as if she were tired, and said, "I'll talk to you later," and walked back to her own stoop.

"You work for *Crime Scene?*" Janie Hobson asked.

"Yeah. I'm doing a story on your ex-husband."

"Brownie made *Crime Scene?*" Janie Hobson said, "Lord, he'd have killed himself for that."

Taylor watched a couple of local politicians he recognized walk into the Roumanian Grill down at the corner. As the door opened, the sound of the music the girls danced to floated out into the air. From time to time, Taylor had to spend an evening in there chasing a story. The Roumanian was the most popular night club on the Lower East Side. Politicians and show business people packed it every night, so Taylor had wound up doing more than a few interviews at its bar. Abe Haimowitz, the 300 pound maniac who ran the place, called himself the Mayor of Forsyth Street.

"Brownie liked publicity?"

"Oh, yeah. A national magazine like yours? He'd have done anything. You don't understand, Mr....?"

He'd already told her his name once. "Taylor. Damon Taylor."

"Well, Mr. Taylor, you just don't understand about Brownie. There was nothing he loved as much as seeing himself in the papers. Any mention of his name puffed him up like a blowfish. Didn't matter if the story was good or bad, as long as it was in print. If his picture was there, too, he didn't touch the ground for a week."

Hobson's widow was a small woman with bleached blonde hair and huge round eyes. She wore a plain blue skirt that was a little faded out and a white blouse that didn't a thing for her complexion. It looked to Taylor as if she didn't plan to leave the block this morning; she had no makeup on and her hair was pulled back into a bun. She looked tired. Taylor figured that when Brownie started making money, none of it went to his ex-wife. She lived on the second floor of a tenement above a fish shop across the street.

"Liked publicity, did he?"

"Brownie didn't want a thing in this life but to be important. His goal was to be a big man. It was pathetic, really."

It was routine, Taylor told himself. You wanted to know why something happened to a person, you looked at his life. You took a look at who he was, where he came from, who he associated with, what his dreams and desires were, all of that. Where a man wound up came out of where he began. If what he wants is not good for him, where he winds up usually isn't going to be worth a damn either. He listened and made notes, adding sympathetic comments every once in a while.

"Did you know that when we formed the group, I was his partner? He danced with me" she said.

"You said when *we* formed the group. You were in on the original idea?"

"In on it? It was my idea from the beginning. I was dancing in clubs and I saw all that swing stuff going on, saw how popular it was, and I told Brownie we could make some money putting together a swing troupe."

"Then it's really your group?"

"Should have been. Should be. But it isn't and never will be now. The truth is I'm a pretty good dancer, maybe better than pretty good, but as soon as the group started getting regular gigs, he threw me out, replaced me with some little tramp. Only took him a couple of months to replace me in his life, too. You know what he told me?"

"No," he said.

About ten feet away, in front of the stairs that led up to the el, a peddler was selling slices of watermelon for a nickel apiece. Kids ran to their mothers, begging for change, and then charged over to trade in their coins for slices. The kids who weren't buying fruit were spending their money on gelati, which a guy on the corner across the street was peddling out of a pushcart. While a chubby little boy who wasn't wearing a shirt looked on eagerly, the peddler loaded a paper cup with ice and covered it with flavored syrup. Taylor remembered gelati from his own childhood and wondered if he'd still find one delicious.

"He said they were working uptown now and he looked at me like I was something from behind the counter in that fish shop over there and said, 'you ain't uptown, baby.'"

"What did you do?"

"What could I do? I let him go uptown."

"You divorced him?"

"Who'd want to hold onto a man like him? Let's face it, Mr. Taylor, he never was much of a husband anyway."

"You seem to have some pretty strong feelings, Mrs. Hobson."

"Strong enough to kill him, you mean?"

"I've got no reason to accuse you," he said.

"I'd never kill him," she said. "I'd hurt him, maybe break his legs so he couldn't dance, cut off his thing so he couldn't run around on any woman ever again, but I wouldn't kill him. That would end his suffering and, let me tell you, Mr. Taylor, I never had any interest in ending his suffering."

When Taylor walked over toward Second Avenue to catch a bus back uptown, a man who'd been lingering in the doorway of the Roumanian Grill strolled across the street casually, as if he had nothing on his mind. His hands were tucked in his pockets. He had short blonde hair and deep-set eyes that appeared to be amused by the world. His suit jacket was buttoned, cut in a modified zoot suit fashion.

"Mrs. Hobson?"

"Yes?"

She didn't like the looks of the man who was staring down at her. Maybe he thought of his grin as careless and charming, she thought, but to her it was scary as a Peter Lorre movie. His expression signaled that he had something on everybody, as though he walked a few feet above the surface of the earth and dared anyone to question it. She'd seen that look before on the people who owned or managed the night clubs she used to work in and one thing she could say for sure, familiarity did not breed comfort.

"That guy that just left?" he asked. "Who was he?"

"I don't think that's any of your business, Mr....?"

"Francesca. Mannie Francesca."

"Well, Mr. Francesca, like I said, I'm not sure..."

He interrupted her. "Oh, come on, Mrs. Hobson, don't you think it'd be easier if you just told me what I want to know, if you just gave me his name and told me what he was asking about? I mean, we both know you're going to wind up telling me, don't we?"

"You frighten me."

He flashed that grin again. "That being the case, the best thing you can do is tell me what I want to know so I can go away and you won't have to be scared anymore."

That made sense to her. She did what he asked.

"Managed the Lindy Hoppers?" Ronnie Hamilton said with a shocked expression. "I didn't manage them, man. I *made* the Lindy Hoppers. I'm the Lindy Hoppers' daddy." He leaned forward, resting his palms on the top of his desk. "When I met those kids, they were green, and they were being eaten alive by a manager who was so damn totally inept, it's a wonder they could land a gig. See, Brownie himself was running the show. He thought he could do everything. All he did was create more resentment than you could shake a stick at. Club owners, bookers, they all hated him. Hell, even the kids in the troupe hated him. He hired 'em, rehearsed 'em, paid 'em, fired 'em. He got the gigs and took the lion's share of the money. He took fifty percent, the rest of the group split the other fifty."

"Why'd they put up with it?"

"You're a guy that jitterbugs for a living, how many job opportunities you got?"

"See what you mean. Still, the Lindy Hoppers were working steady, weren't they?"

"Oh, sure, they were working, all right. Every night."

"Look, if Brownie's doing that good, why'd he need you?"

He was willing to bet that Ronnie Hamilton was a name that came from a lot of thought and study, that it was a show business choice. What he was looking at was a Jewish guy who had, like Winchell, Jack Benny, George Burns and a thousand others, made a decision to adopt a more goyish name, in order to crash through to big time show biz. He couldn't say it was a bad move but you wouldn't think it was still necessary.

The nation had fought a war for freedom, but when he looked around, Taylor didn't see a hell of a lot of freedom. What he saw was people who'd come home assuming that the fight had been won, only to discover that it had just taken a more subtle turn; the battlefields were harder to locate, that's all.

Enough to make a man cynical.

If you were already cynical, it was enough to make you sound like some kind of pompous preacher.

Hamilton lit a cigar. It took him a few moments to get it started. "Why'd he need me? Because he was doing all those things and he wasn't worth a damn at any of them. What you got to realize is Brownie Hobson was only good at two things: dancing and throwing drunks out of bars. Here was a guy that could barely read the contracts he was signing. I'm telling you, the booking agents loved to see him coming. The agents would negotiate a price with a club and give Brownie maybe half of it. Fifty percent commission." He had a longing look in his eye. "Can you imagine that? Christ, he had to have a guy with a brain on his side."

"And that was you?"

"Damn right it was me. You think he could have gotten himself into the movies? You think he could have booked himself into the Savoy?"

A thin scar ran down Hamilton's right cheek. Unless you looked carefully, you'd think it was just a skin crease. Taylor made a note to check Hamilton's background.

"He have any enemies?"

"Another thing you got to realize was that he wasn't a very popular guy. Back in the early days, hell, up till about six months ago, he used to moonlight between gigs as muscle for some loan shark. It wasn't like he needed the money. He just liked the work. I had to stop him before he hurt the act."

"Who'd he work for?"

"I couldn't tell you."

"You can't tell me or you don't know?"

"Don't matter, does it? Either way I ain't telling you."

The man behind the desk was well-muscled but carried a little too much fat on his body. He was careful to wear suits that he thought hid his bulk. He looked up as Mannie Francesca tossed a copy of *Crime Scene* onto the desk.

"Did you see this?"

The man behind the desk wore a white shirt with the collar open and his red and black striped tie loosened. He picked up the magazine and checked out the cover.

Flipping through the pages, he said, "There a reason why I might be interested in this?"

"They're writing about Brownie Hobson."

"That a fact?" the man behind the desk said.

He made no attempt to hide the fact that he was balding. His remaining hair was swept back, pomaded so that it looked as though it were molded to the side of his head, which appeared to be too big for his body. His face was round, with small, deep-set eyes.

"Yeah," Francesca said. "They're playing the story up pretty good."

"What are they saying?"

"The guy talks about the shooting, talks about Hobson's life and then makes a couple of guesses about the shooting."

"And you're calling this to my attention for what reason?"

Mannie Francesca wiped sweat from his forehead. Although there was a chair next to the desk, he continued to stand. He shifted his weight from foot to foot. When he wiped sweat from his face again, his biceps flexed and tightening the material of the suit. His face looked as though it had taken some punches.

"Well, thing is, they say Brownie's got ties to organized crime."

"They say this?"

"Well, it's more like they hint at it."

"I see," the man said, taking a pack of Philip Morrises out of his pocket. Shaking out a cigarette, he tapped it on his thumbnail before putting it into his mouth. He held the match in front of the cigarette without lighting it. "Who wrote it?"

"Guy named Damon Taylor."

"You know him?"

The big man shook his head.

"Tell you what: why don't you go out and find out who this guy is, what he knows?"

Francesca rubbed his right fist. "Can I hurt him?"

"Not yet. Not unless you absolutely have to."

"Okay, then." He smiled. "I'll put a couple of guys on it."

The man behind the desk held a hand up. "If he's a threat to us, I want to know about it."

"I don't understand it," Linda said. "Remember when you were telling me about the witnesses in the Savoy? How they all said things that canceled each other out? It sounds like we got another case of that. From what you tell me, the man's a gangster who's a saint, a criminal genius who can't do anything but beat people up, a devoted husband who deserted two wives—it doesn't make sense."

They were sitting along the first base line at Ebbets Field. There was never a problem getting good seats at the ball park; no matter how good a team the Dodgers fielded, they couldn't draw more than a few thousand people. You could buy a bleacher seat and then just walk down and sit anywhere you wanted. The Yankees and the Giants both drew well, but Brooklyn couldn't generate a crowd if they gave away a free beach vacation to every paying customer.

It was a pleasant afternoon, the heat having finally broken and the Dodgers were warming up on the field. The game would start at 3:15 after the stock market had closed for the day so that the Wall Street guys would have time to ride the subway out to Brooklyn. He watched Jackie Robinson lope easily across the outfield, catching fly balls.

"That's the way it goes," Taylor said. "Everybody tells you about the man who lived in their head, not the guy who lived in the city."

"I suppose," Linda said. She studied the players as they warmed up. "You know, baseball's just not the same now that Babe Ruth's dead."

Ruth had died back during the winter and Linda was right; a pall hung over all three stadiums. Even if he hadn't been active as a player for a long time, the Babe had been the living symbol of baseball in the city. A few years back, he'd done a stretch as a batting coach for the Dodgers and every once in a while he'd pick up a bat and put on a show for the crowds. He might have weighed close to 300 pounds and been so totally out of shape that he could barely walk anymore, but he could still whack one out of the park. People in the bars chattered about the possibility of a comeback until the day he died.

Without him around, the players all looked a little smaller.

With two outs in the first inning, Enos Slaughter beat out a single and Stan Musial came to the plate. Linda leaned forward in her seat. "I should hate him," she said, "for what he does to the Dodgers, but how can you hate a man that hits as well as he does?"

Two men appeared in the row behind them and stood directly in back of Taylor. Their shadow fell over him. He sensed them there and, when they did not sit down, felt the hairs on his arm rise. He hadn't expected anyone to come after him this soon.

"Taylor," one of them said.

He turned. The two men had on suits with loose jackets that they kept buttoned, so Taylor knew they were carrying guns beneath them. He frowned. It was way too early in the Hobson story for anybody to be upset. Who were these guys and what did they want?

"I'm Taylor."

"We need to talk. Maybe you wouldn't mind coming with us a minute?"

"I don't think so. Musial's up."

Musial hit a long drive out to left field that Gene Hermanski chased down and caught. It was a tough play but Hermanski made it seem routine. Taylor mentally saluted him.

"Musial's not up anymore. Let's go talk."

"Be back in a minute, Linda."

She watched them walk up the steps toward the concession stand. The two men placed themselves on each side of Taylor, closer to him than they needed to be, as if they were holding him in place. She didn't have a good feeling about this. When they reached the top of the stairs, she decided to follow, to see what they were up to.

When they reached the men's room, one of the men cast a quick glance around. He saw that no one was watching, so he nodded to the other one. They shoved Taylor into the room.

"Jesus," the smaller one said, "smells like an asshole in here."

Taylor wondered who these two were. He knew one thing; they weren't mobbed up. Their clothes were too conservative—dark suits, white shirts and understated ties—and not as expensive as the out-fits the mobsters usually wore. The one who seemed to be the leader had short hair, so evenly blonde that it looked died. He smiled as though he thought something that only he understood was funny and held his hands in front of him as if he were either praying or anticipating a fine meal. His partner looked as if he'd just had a hair-cut that morning. He still smelled of cologne.

It happened fast. The blonde one nodded to his friend who, moving more quickly than Taylor could have imagined, grabbed his arms, pulling them back and pinning them behind Taylor's back, while the blonde guy, still smiling, stepped forward and hit him in the stomach. Taylor felt the breath rush from his lungs and gasped as the fist slammed into his stomach again and again like a piston. This guy had done this before, Taylor thought; he was very good at throwing a punch and damned if he wasn't having a good time doing it. When the blonde man got tired of hitting him in the stomach, he slammed him in the face a few times and then signaled his partner.

"That's enough," he said.

His partner released Taylor, who slumped to the floor. No more than a minute had gone by. God, what if they'd been somewhere private, where they'd have all the time they needed?

"My guess is," the blonde man said, "I don't have to tell you why we did that." When Taylor didn't answer, he continued, "You're on the verge of walking through some doors you don't want to enter. Drop the Hobson story."

The other guy added, "What you want to keep in mind is we could have just as easily killed you."

As they walked out of the rest room, Taylor, fighting for consciousness, found himself wondering once again just who these two guys were. He couldn't hold the thought in his mind, though; the pain kept driving it out.

10

"Damn," O'Bradovich said, handing Taylor a fresh ice pack, "they really did a job on you."

Taylor slumped on his couch, his shirt off, holding the ice pack to his eye, which, swollen almost shut, throbbed steadily, painfully. His ribs hurt so badly that he wondered if they were broken. Already bruises were forming on his rib cage.

"Get him a drink," Linda said.

Taylor nodded. Speaking took too much effort. When O'Bradovich brought him a glass of whiskey, he took it in his free hand and tossed it down. He looked up at Linda and O'Bradovich, saw the worry in their faces and figured he must look like hell. He ought to get a glance of himself in the mirror, but he wasn't sure how well he could move. He also wasn't in a hurry to see the shape the two guys had left him in. He could feel it. That was enough.

"Get me some aspirin?" he said. His voice was thick.

"Damon," Linda said, "are you sure you don't want to go to the emergency room?"

"I'm okay. Just need some aspirin."

"Aspirin. The taxi driver had to haul him up the stairs and he thinks aspirin's going to do the job. Bob, can't you do anything with this guy?"

"It's all right. Thanks for taking care of me."

"Seriously, Damon, those guys beat you up pretty good."

"They were pros. They didn't break anything."

"What?"

"Messing me up wasn't the plan. Sending me a message was."

The evening humidity filled the air with moisture that the fan couldn't cut. All it did was push the wet air around the room. Taylor could feel sweat trickling down his ribcage.

"Yeah, well, I can see that damn message all over your face."

"Like the man said, they could have just as easily killed me."

Pulling himself to his feet, he figured it was time to get it over with and walked clumsily, staggering just enough to upset Linda, into the bathroom, where he checked himself out in the mirror. A huge purple bruise had formed under his right eye and his lip was split. "I look like hell, don't I?"

"You say this was sending you a message?" Linda said.

"That's right"

"What's the message?"

"Drop the Hobson story."

"This has something to do with Brownie Hobson?"

"Yeah."

Linda shook her head. "What's going on? He was a dancer, that's all. I mean, I'm sorry he's dead and everything, but you can't say he was some important guy. He wasn't somebody who'd get people this angry, was he?"

"Christ, they didn't beat the hell out of me because they don't want to see a profile of Big Joe Turner printed. No, it's Brownie Hobson, all right. They told me to get off the story."

"They beat the hell out of you to warn you off the story?"

He was walking more easily now, so he made his way to the kitchen and poured himself another drink. This time he added ice cubes; warm whiskey was a disgrace. Feeling weak, he sat heavily at the kitchen table, hoping Linda didn't notice the way he'd damn near collapsed.

"Somebody either thinks I know something or they must be afraid I'm going to find something out."

"But what?" O'Bradovich said. He sat opposite Taylor and freshened his own drink.

"That's the thing. I got no idea."

"So what are you going to do?"

"Only thing I can. Start over from the beginning. Either I'm overlooking something or I'm not nearly as close as somebody thinks I am."

"Let me see if I understand this," O'Bradovich said. "Two hoodlums accost you in a public place, a ball park..."

"The way the Dodgers draw, I'm not sure you can call Ebbets Field a public place."

"Very funny. Two hoodlums take you into a public rest room, beat the living hell out of you, and it makes no impression on you at all?"

"Oh, it's going to make me a little more careful, I can flat out guarantee you that, but Bob, what you have to understand is you don't get scared off a story. You just can't let that happen."

"Oh, I see. For the sake of a slight to your manhood, you're going to take a chance on them killing you next time."

The rain that had been threatening all afternoon started to fall. It was heavy, with a wind that blew it into the apartment. O'Bradovich closed the windows while Linda turned the fan up to high. Taylor watched them; they operated like some sort of well-trained, efficient weather crew.

"Nobody's going to kill me," he said. "If they'd wanted me dead, they would have killed me this afternoon."

"Oh," Linda said, "So they're just going to beat you up again?"

Taylor walked over to the closet. From the top shelf, he took a towel and unfolded it. Inside was the .45 automatic he'd brought home from the war. It would have to be cleaned and oiled but, what the hell, he'd done that before.

"Nobody's going to beat me up again," he said.

Linda frowned at the gun and started to say something. Stopping, she shook her head as though she were disgusted. "I hope to hell," she said, "you know what you're doing."

"Don't worry about it."

"Damon, you're frightening me."

"Damn it, Linda, I'm the one that's supposed to be scared."

"And aren't you?"

"I've been through worse than this."

"Damon, the war's over, all right?" Her voice was loud, tight. "Can't you get that? You don't bring the war home with you."

"Jesus, you got no idea who these guys were?" Marsczyk said.

"None."

"Whoever they were, they ain't amateurs, are they? They did a hell of a job on you."

"Glad you like it."

On Marsczyk's TV set, Tex and Jinx chatted with some nightclub singer that Taylor didn't recognize. While he'd been overseas, a whole new set of show business people had come along. He didn't know who anybody was any more. O'Bradovich kept him up to date on Broadway and radio people, but in every other area, he was back in the thirties. The fact was, though, he didn't much give a damn.

"You got any idea why?"

"Let's go with the obvious. Brownie's involved in something big enough to get him killed. Somebody figures I either know what it is or I'm going to find out. They don't want to see whatever the hell it is in print."

"And what have you found out?"

"Not a damn thing."

"You know what that means. Don't you?"

"What?"

"You know something you don't know you know." Marsczyk leaned back, his feet on the desk, hands clasped behind his head.

"Say that again."

"You know what I'm saying, Bright Eyes. You stumbled on something and you aren't aware what it is or how important it is yet." He smiled, enjoying this process. "Let's go over what you got."

"Okay, Brownie's a bouncer who formed a dance troupe. Jitterbug, you know? You can't really call it a dance troupe. They jump around, toss the girls over their backs. It's about as close to dancing as Sonny Tufts is to acting."

"Don't editorialize. Bouncer, huh? Where'd he work?"

"I know where you're going with this. He worked clubs, so we got to figure at the very least he knows some mob guys."

"Don't get ahead of yourself. You say he worked clubs. Which ones? For how long? Who'd he associate with in them?"

"I haven't gone that far back."

"Try it. See if anything surfaces." He rubbed his fingertips as though clicking off ideas. "Now you said he knows some mob guys. Which ones? And exactly how well does he know them?"

"He knew them well enough that they sent a couple of guys after me today."

"We don't know that."

"Oh? The bruises don't convince you?"

"Hell, man, I believe you got beat up, sure. I just don't know it was mobsters that did it."

"I remember thinking at the time they were too well dressed for mob muscle."

"You got enough style sense to know when somebody's well dressed?" He ran his eyes slowly over Taylor's suit. "Where the hell did that come from?"

"Funny. But if it wasn't mob guys, who was it?"

"I don't know. Go find out." He clicked his fingers again. "You've checked Hobson's associations, then?"

"Not completely. I got my ass kicked before I could get it done."

He hit the interoffice intercom. "Doris, you want to bring me and Taylor some coffee?" Turning to Taylor, he said, "You're going to want to see who he was close to."

Whenever Taylor was stuck on a story, he sat down with Marsczyk, who, since he had no personal involvement in anything, always had a fresh perspective on a story. Taylor always came away from these sessions energized, with a new set of possibilities.

"You know what bothers me?" he said.

Doris brought in a couple of cups of coffee. Marsczyk added three lumps of sugar to his, then followed it up with cream. Taylor took his black.

"What bothers you?"

"The fact that you might be right. I'm having more and more a hard time taking these guys for mob talent, but I can't figure out who else would be involved in this."

"What do you mean?"

"They weren't the type. For one thing, they looked educated."

"Again, what do you mean?"

He took a sip of coffee, careful to keep it away from his split lip. It was a little sharp, had been on the burner too long. Still, he enjoyed it. He knew better than to take a cup of coffee for granted; he'd gone all across Europe without tasting a good cup.

"They spoke well, had a basic knowledge of the way grammar works, you know?"

Marsczyk raised his eyebrows. "See what you mean. Is that all?"

"No accents."

"Maybe you were gone too long. The mobs are changing. It ain't all Sicilian anymore."

"I guess."

The sun broke through the clouds, filtering in through the window, brightening the room. Taylor smiled; the leg work was going to be easier without the threat of more rain.

"So what are you going to do now?"

"I'm wondering where they picked me up. It must have been from somebody I talked to. Now, the question is, did somebody rat me out?"

"Why don't you go find out?"

"That's what I got in mind."

11

McCall took one look at Taylor's face and whistled. "You might not want to spend any time around little kids for a while."

"Thanks for being so concerned."

"Any time."

They were strolling through Washington Square Park. The afternoon was pleasant, a warm breeze rustling the leaves. McCall was eating an ice cream cone and he stopped to watch a couple of old men playing chess. When they had stared at the board without moving a piece for close to five minutes, he walked on.

"Knight to Bishop was the move," he said.

"I'll take your word for it," Taylor said, "Listen, I need to know if you've got anything I haven't."

"From the look of your face, I guess you do."

"This thing's getting out of hand and I don't know why."

"Or how."

"That, too."

Over near the arch, a folksinger who looked like he'd never been beyond Brooklyn strummed a nylon string guitar and sang about life on the chain gang. The group of adoring young girls around him loved it, but it only made Taylor want to walk faster. Ahead of him, a trio played banjos and guitars, loudly, badly.

"Ought to pass a law against these guys," McCall said.

"Public nuisance?"

"Threat to Goddamn civilization is more like it. Can't even enjoy the park anymore. Everywhere you look there's a damn folksinger."

"Not your favorite music, huh?"

"Music? You call that crap music?"

"Some of it's good. Look, you got anything on the Hobson case?"

McCall shot him a look. Chewing on his cone, he said through a full mouth, "Not a damn thing. For all I got, it might as well have been a suicide." He dropped the rest of the cone in a trash can. "You got more than I have."

"I do?"

"Got yourself beat up, didn't you?"

"Yeah, but I don't know who did it or why."

"Do me a favor. When you find out, let me know."

"You can't give me a direction?"

"'Fraid not. If I had any kind of a lead, I'd give it to you. God knows I got no time to follow up on it. I'm working a dozen cases."

"Anything interesting?"

"Nothing that rates *Crime Scene*. Woman killed her cheating husband, but, hell, that ain't even news anymore. Shooting in the Garment District. Everything's routine."

"Any of them develop into anything, you'll let me know?"

"Sure. You do the same on the Hobson thing."

On their way out of the park, they passed the folksinger again. He was doing a twelve bar blues about not having a home, having to wander down the highways with his dog.

Yes, sir, Taylor thought, sing what you know.

Terri Louvin lived in the Village. Her apartment was in the basement of a brownstone on Jane Street and when she opened the door to Taylor's knock, she had an exhausted expression on her face, as if she hadn't been sleeping well for a week or so. She'd slapped on some makeup to try to conceal the puffy bags beneath her eyes but it hadn't worked.

"You're Taylor?"

"Thanks for seeing me," he said.

"You might as well come on in but try to keep your voice down, okay? I had a hell of a time getting Danny down for his nap."

"You've got a kid?"

"Eight months old."

"Must make it hard to do dance gigs."

She flashed a quick smile, but couldn't sustain it. "It does. When the group was working, I was spending just about everything I made on baby sitting."

The wall of the room was mirrored, with a ballet bar at waist height. To say the room was sparsely furnished was to exaggerate. A beat up arm chair sat in the corner. Opposite it, at the far end of the room, were a couple of bar stools. A very expensive Capehart radio-phonograph, the Imperial model with the Flip-o-Matic record changer—he recognized it because Linda owned the exact same model—sat on the far end of the room, up against the wall that was not mirrored, as the one opposite was. The radio was tuned to a classical station but was turned down so low he could barely hear it.

"You know, this doesn't look like a swing dancer's place."

"It isn't. Swing pays the bills, Mr. Taylor. Well, it used to, at least. I'm a ballerina. I still study. Well, up till…" she hesitated. "You know."

He nodded. "That's why I'm here, Miss Louvin…"

"Please, call me Terri."

"Terri. And I'm Damon."

"Nice name."

"Thanks. Look, you know I'm covering Brownie's murder for *Crime Scene*."

She shuddered. "It was the most horrible thing I've ever seen." She closed her eyes, as if she were trying to avoid seeing the scene again. "You know, I didn't even realize what was happening. We were dancing, we'd just started and Brownie was reaching for me, getting ready to do the first spin, and suddenly blood started spurting out of his belly and I heard this series of, I don't know, it didn't sound anything like gunshots do in the movies, you know, it was just this series of popping sounds, real flat, and Brownie just collapsed with this horrible expression on his face."

"Did you see the people that shot him?"

"I never looked at anything but Brownie. When he fell, I just dropped down next to him. I don't know, maybe I was in shock, maybe I thought I could help him. He's all I was looking at."

"I know it's hard for you. Thanks for going through it again." He tapped his pen on his pad. "You don't have any idea why it happened?"

"None."

"What had Brownie been up to the couple of days before it happened? Would you have any way of knowing?"

Glancing down at the floor shyly, she smiled. "Why, you don't know, do you?"

"Know what?"

"Damon, Brownie lived here. He was my boyfriend."

"Oh. No, I didn't know."

"We've been together for two years, since he and his wife broke up."

He noticed she'd slipped into present tense. She sat in the middle of the floor, legs crossed in front of her, elbows on her knees, chin resting in her hands. She looked gamine-like, but everything, all of her gestures, all of her movements, were exaggerated, larger than life. Had he seen her on the street, Taylor would have immediately spotted her as a dancer, but not a ballerina. She had the looks and overblown personality of the Broadway chorus girls O'Bradovich was always going out with. Taylor was certain that was where her career would lead her.

"He's your son's father?"

Terri nodded and smiled. "Sure is." Then her face changed, closed off and grew dark. "Was, I mean. Jesus, Damon, I don't know what we're going to do." She fought back tears, her head tossing in small, quick, jerking motions. "I don't know how we're going to keep going."

He waited silently. There was nothing he could say. He used to find himself wishing for some set of magic words he could say that would wash away pain, but the past few years in slugging his way from Africa through Italy into Germany had shown him there weren't any. Taylor sat silently on the bar stool as he watched her fight for control.

She forced a smile and said, "I'm sorry."

"Nothing to apologize for."

"I get a little worried. We never made a lot of money, you know? Specialty acts don't. I mean, we got by. Between the two of us, we brought home enough to stay afloat, you understand, but now, with Brownie gone..."

"Brownie's manager said he was doing pretty good."

"If he was, he wasn't bringing any of it home. No, Damon, we were struggling. Getting the rent together every month was tough." She shook her head again. "I don't know what I'm going to do."

"It'll be okay."

"Sure," she tried to smile. "I'll pick up some gigs."

"The troupe isn't going to go on?"

"Oh, hell, that idiot Frankie DeMarco says he's going to take it over, but the only thing he can run is his mouth. He'll never be able to keep a dance troupe afloat." She tried another smile. "Maybe it's for the best. The group disbanding, I mean. It's time I got back to doing real dancing."

"You mind if I ask a couple of questions about Brownie?"

"Go ahead."

"I understand he did some freelance work."

"You're talking about the muscle stuff." Her voice was as flat as the bottom of an iron.

"Yeah."

"He didn't want to do it, not anymore. Since Dannie was born," she cut her eyes toward the bedroom where the baby was sleeping, "he wanted to change his ways. Every once in a while, though, we'd need the money real bad and he'd go out at night."

"Who did he work for?"

She looked up at him, helplessness in her eyes. "I don't know. He never wanted to talk about it. I'd ask him about it, but he always said I was better off not knowing."

A symphony came on the radio. It was loud, with a lot of dynamics, so Terri got up, crossed the room and cut the radio off. She stood, staring down at the cabinet for a long time. Then she walked back to the center of the room, but did not sit down again.

"You think that stuff, his 'freelance work,' you called it, might have gotten him killed?"

"I don't know. It's a possibility," Taylor said. "Was he upset about anything?"

"Only about the new costumes," she said with a shrug.

"What do you mean?"

"Oh, he went down to see the designer who was doing our new costumes one day last week and came home pretty upset. I asked what was bothering him, but he wouldn't talk about it. Said it was business and I shouldn't worry my pretty little face about it. I figured the guy wanted more money or something. Brownie was always getting upset over money."

"Who was doing the costumes?"

She glanced at his reflection in the mirror. "What difference does that make? You don't get killed over a costume."

"I don't know if it makes any difference at all. I'm just trying to walk through the past couple of weeks, that's all. See if I can find anything."

"The jobber was Simon Haynes."

"Jobber?"

"He's the guy that designs the costumes, finds the cloth, the accessories and oversees the construction."

"I thought the designer did that."

"Most of the time, designers don't do a thing. They make little sketches, turn them over to jobbers and then approve the final product. No, the jobber's the man."

"And this Haynes is the guy you used?"

"He does great dance costumes."

Taylor wrote down the name. "Is he the owner of the shop? Will I find it under his name?"

"No, he works for Vera Kelly. Look, the thing you have to understand is he's a friend of Brownie's. He did our costumes under the table. Don't get him in any trouble."

"I won't. Anything else you can think of?"

"No, I'm afraid not."

"You sure you don't have a name on the muscle stuff?"

"I heard him on the phone a few times, talking to a guy he called Leo. Just about every time, when he got off the phone, he said he had to go out to work."

"You don't know this guy Leo?"

She shook her head. "Never met him. I don't even know if it's his first or last name."

"If you think of anything else that can help, will you give me a call?" He handed her one of his *Crime Scene* business cards.

She read the card. "Sure."

"Listen, you need any money or anything?"

She touched his forearm lightly. "I'll be fine."

"You need anything, you call me, okay?"

She shook her head slowly back and forth. "Why are you being so generous? You don't even know me."

"It's not a big deal." He felt embarrassed, off-center.

"So, what, you're some kind of Good Samaritan magazine writer, just going around writing about dead people and helping out the widows you don't know from Adam?"

"You make it sound weird."

"Mister, in this city, it is weird."

12

"Leo, huh?" Truman Capote said.

It was quarter after ten and they were in a booth at Costello's. The morning papers would be put to bed soon and the place would be mobbed, but right now, only a few men hung out at the bar, talking baseball. One of them, a small, round-shouldered guy in his fifties who looked like he was bitter because he'd never made it off the rewrite desk, was still upset because Branch Rickey had signed Jackie Robinson last season. The other two were pointing out to him that Robinson had made the Dodgers into a baseball team again.

Capote shot a glance at them. "You figure the racial talk is going to start in a minute?"

"Any time now."

"It always does. That Jackie Robinson's a lightning rod, isn't he? I tell you, Damon, I hate that stuff. I'm from Alabama, you know? I heard that sort of talk all my life."

"We could go over and slap him silly."

"Damon, have you taken a good look at me? Do you think I'm the one to slap anybody silly?"

"I was joking."

Capote looked across the booth at Taylor, his face drawn, serious, as though he'd put in too many long nights. "I know you were. Still, you could pull it off. You've got a mean look about you, like you know how to dish it out. People are intimidated by you. Me, it's all they can do not to giggle."

Even though Capote was correct, Taylor felt he should say something to make the kid feel better. "Don't be so tough on yourself." It was the best he could do.

"I'm not. I'm just being realistic, that's all."

The kid looked like he'd been burning the candle pretty seriously. It wasn't so much as if he'd been burning it at both ends, it was more like he'd made a bonfire out of it. He'd either been working too hard or partying too hard; either way Capote was drinking too much. Taylor thought it was pretty much a matter of time before he exploded.

Terry Porter came in, waved to them and, after grabbing a drink, strolled casually and a touch unsteadily over to the booth. "Taylor, Capote," he nodded in their general direction, "how you boys doing?" This wasn't Porter's first stop of the evening. He was unsure on his feet and sat heavily, his drink spilling over onto his wrist. Like a cat, he licked the wrist clean. His suit was wrinkled, with a dirty spot on the lapel, and his tie hung askew. Somewhere along the way he'd lost his hat.

"Just the man I was looking for," Taylor said.

Why was everybody drinking so much tonight? Not that boozing it up was so unusual. Since the war ended, everybody was drinking too much, but it was too early in the evening for Porter or anyone else to be that drunk.

"That a fact? I been kind of hard to find tonight, man. Been doing the town pretty good."

"I can see that." He pulled his own drink closer, as though he were afraid that Porter would grab it. "Anything wrong?"

"Wrong? Hell, man, what could possibly be wrong?" He looked like he'd eaten something delicious.

"If you're fine," Capote said, "I'd hate to see somebody that's suffering."

"My judgment is being questioned by a dwarf." Porter looked at Capote as if he were an interesting plant. "Damon, you think that's right?"

"No need to talk like that, Terry. He's just trying to help."

"Big Time, my girl friend's husband, the one she said she didn't have, showed up today. He came to my place, looking for her. How the hell he knew to come there's way the hell beyond me, but the knock came at the door, I opened it and here's this old white haired guy from Louisiana looking for his wife, who just happens to be my girl friend, who never bothered to tell me she already had a husband. A guy old enough to be her father. The way he talked? Makes that drawl of Capote's sound normal. Had an accent so thick I couldn't understand a word he was saying." He hesitated, taking a deep breath. "Till he said my girl friend's name, that is, and told me he was her husband." He pointed his whiskey-soaked hand at Capote. "So what do you say you just keep your observations about how I look to yourself and get me another drink?"

Capote, who had been taking notes, closed his notebook and scurried over to the bar. While he was gone, Taylor tried to settle Porter down. It was like stroking an irritable cat; at first he'd snarl at you, try to bite your fingers but gradually he'd relax in spite of himself. By the time Capote brought the fresh round back, Porter was under control again.

"Reason I was looking for you, Terry," Taylor said, "is I need a little help. Brownie was still doing muscle work now and then, when things were tight. Most of the time he worked for a guy named Leo."

"And we don't know who this Leo is, huh?" Porter said. His voice was thick, his diction slurred, but now that he had a problem to focus on, he suddenly became more alert.

"That's right."

"That's all you got? A first name?"

"If it's even a first name. Not much, is it?"

Capote said, "Maybe it's Leo Salmon. You know, the money collector for Huey Malgoni."

Taylor and Porter exchanged looks. Porter picked up his drink and looked at it as though he were trying to guess its age. Then he took a long swallow and shivered the way Capote had earlier.

"You know, of course," Porter said, "the significance of what you're saying?"

"What do you mean?"

"Like you said, Leo Salmon works for Huey Malgoni. Huey Malgoni worked for Louis Lepke."

"So?"

"Louis Lepke was in business with Frank Costello."

"I don't understand what you're getting at."

"You're suggesting that Brownie used to free lance as muscle for the most organized of organized crime." Turning to Taylor, he added, "Although we all know there's no such thing as organized crime because J. Edgar Hoover told us so."

"Yeah, and he says Frank Costello is a sportsman."

"Is it so unlikely that this Brownie person would be working for Salmon?" Capote said.

"Very."

"You've also got to consider that we're jumping to conclusions here," Taylor said. "There's a million Leos in this town. The odds of Salmon being the one might be kind of remote."

"Not that remote," Capote said. "Leo Salmon was at Brownie's funeral."

"He was? How do you know that?"

Capote shrugged. "I was there."

"You recognized him?"

"Oh, no. How would I possibly be able to recognize him? I'd never seen him before. I spoke to him at the cemetery."

"You spoke to him."

Porter seemed to suddenly believe that Capote had just arrived from some other planet. He wore an incredulous expression that Taylor had never seen before. He'd stare at Capote, look away and shake his head, and then stare again.

"Oh, yes. We had a nice talk."

"You went to Brownie's funeral? I didn't know you even knew him," Porter said. His voice was tentative.

"I didn't. Never met him."

"But you went to his funeral?"

He shrugged. "I was working on a story that has a funeral in it."

"So you figured you'd just go out and attend a stranger's funeral for research."

"I'm not sure you could call him a stranger. After all, Damon, I read your piece on him."

"Oh, well, that makes all the difference."

"How do you expect me to write about a New York funeral if I've never seen one?"

Porter leaned forward, clasped Capote's hand in both of his and said, "It's fiction, Capote, make it up."

The man following Taylor wore a tan hat that did not go with his dark suit. The hat was light enough to pick up a reflection from the street lamps, so that he might as well have been wearing a lantern on his head. Still, probably because Taylor was half in the bag and sleepy, it took him three blocks to pick the tail up. When he noticed the man, he made an unnecessary turn and walked a few blocks. The man hung back half a block on the other side of the street and followed, never letting the distance between them get any greater.

As Taylor entered up the subway, the man in the tan hat got into the next car and hung from a strap so that he could watch the doors.

When Taylor reached his stop, they both headed for the exit. The man in the tan hat tried to mix it up by walking up the opposite set of stairs but he was pretty obvious about it. He picked Taylor up again when they reached Broadway and followed him home.

Inside his apartment, Taylor shot a glance through the window. The man in the tan hat hung around on the street long enough to make sure Taylor wasn't leaving his apartment again that night and then walked slowly back toward the subway.

He'd be back in the morning, Taylor figured.

13

Taylor had guessed right. In the morning, the man in the dark suit, still wearing his tan hat, was back. Now he carried a *Journal-American* folded under his arm. Taylor strolled down to the Automat and collected a buck's worth of nickels from the bored attendant. He drew two cups of coffee. The spigot was shaped like a lion's head and Taylor wondered why they'd gone for that bit of style and nothing more. It was as though the designers of the automat had fired all of their creative bullets with the lion's heads and had decided on a long nap after that.

Holding his tray carefully in one hand, he popped a few coins into the window slot and lifted the door so he could get a couple of plates of donuts. He carried it all over to the table where the man in the dark suit sat, pretending to casually read the sports pages.

The man looked up when Taylor sat down. For an instant, surprise flickered through his eyes but he brought his reaction under control and said, "Something for you, buddy?"

"You might say so," Taylor said. "I need a meeting with Leo Salmon."

Taylor slid the coffee and donuts across the table to the man, who glanced at them, his face quizzical. After a mental shrug, he picked up one of the donuts and took a bite.

"I'm supposed to know what you're talking about, is that it? I'm supposed to know you?"

"Come on," Taylor said, "we both know the score here. We both know I made you and the game's up. Why don't we just accept that and move on to the next step?"

There was a long pause. The man picked up his tan hat and for a moment Taylor thought he was going to leave, but he just toyed with the brim. He appeared to be on the verge of trying to bluff it out. Then he seemed to think better of it.

"And this next step you're talking about has me going to this Leo guy?" he said.

"That's right."

"Why would I know this person?"

"Because somebody's got you following me and the only name that has surfaced since I began working this story is Leo Salmon."

"Maybe I got no idea what you're talking about."

"Fine. Then go back and tell whoever had you following me that I made you and get off my back."

"Then again, we can suppose I do know this Leo Salmon...."

"Let's go farther. Let's suppose Leo Salmon's the guy that's got you tailing me."

"You're a reporter, right?"

"*Crime Scene* magazine."

"How come you're acting like a detective?"

"I'm on a story, that's all. I want to know what happened to Brownie Hobson."

"You know what happened. He got himself shot." He took a sip of coffee.

"Now, you see, that's just what I'm talking about," Taylor said. "A man gets himself shot, that's not a story. For it to be a story, we need to know a little more about it. Why he got hit, for instance."

"And maybe who did it?"

"That's the cops' job, not mine. Until the cops get somebody, I can't say they did it, you know?"

The man in the tan hat finished off his donut and reached for another one. "That a fact?"

"Yeah."

"Even if finding out all this stuff brings down a little heat on you?" He wiped his mouth with a napkin.

Taylor didn't bother to answer. He sipped his coffee. It was hot and strong, but not particularly good. This morning, he didn't care. It didn't matter. The strength of the stuff was enough.

"Let's suppose I can find somebody who knows this Leo Salmon and pass your request on to him. You realize what's likely to happen, don't you?" He polished off the last donut. "I mean, what's likely to happen to you?"

"Sure. I have a nice chat with Mr. Salmon, we get a few things out in the open, and we both go on to have rich fulfilling lives."

"It doesn't make sense. A song and dance man who liked to beat guys up gets himself shot. We got no leads at all and now a mobster's name surfaces? Why?"

Lou Marsczyk lit a fresh cigar, propped his feet on his desk and stared at the TV screen as if he expected to see an answer there. Taylor paced the office. He didn't have a damn thing new. Leo Salmon wasn't a solid enough lead to even print a rumor about. If Marsczyk couldn't help him find a direction, he was going to have to grind out an update without news and the only thing he hated more than reading one of those stories was writing one. You wasted all your time trying to make it sound as though the steamer was chugging steadily toward Europe when you knew it hadn't even left the dock. Maybe most of their readers, the ones he always pictured moving their lips as they read his pieces, didn't care and maybe it didn't make any real difference, but face it, there was professional pride at stake.

"You pick up extra money beating guys up, maybe you do it for a loan shark. Leo's said to have dabbled in that business. Maybe Brownie was working for him."

"Salmon's big time. He's high up in the Costello family. Why would he have a nobody like Hobson on his payroll? That's the part that doesn't make sense?" Marsczyk said. "Salmon don't need Brownie. What, he's skimming off the top of Brownie's dance money? What's he getting out of that? Six, seven bucks a week?"

"Can't go to press without finding out. I'm not about to put Leo in the story as a rumor."

Marszcyk shook his head. "No way in hell. You're dealing with a guy like Leo Salmon, you go to nail it."

A copy boy knocked and opened the door. "Mr. Taylor? Call for you."

Taylor walked over to his desk and picked up the phone.

"A car will be outside your office in fifteen minutes," a voice said. "The driver has instructions to bring you to Mr. Salmon and to bring you safely back. Will that be all right with you?"

"Fine. Fifteen minutes."

Lou Marsczyk was standing next to him when he hung up the phone. "Well?"

"We might have something. I'm meeting with Salmon."

Marsczyk relit his cigar and nodded. Taylor wondered if the fact that his editor didn't speak meant anything. Finally, Marsczyk spoke up.

"You'll be leaving that .45 in my safe, right?"

A black Cadillac waited at the curb, a driver in a chauffeur's uniform leaning against the front fender. He was a young man, no more than twenty-five and his enthusiasm was boundless. He sprung from the fender and opened the door for Taylor. After he'd shut it behind him, he bounced around the car like a puppy, settled behind the wheel and started the engine without using the choke.

"Automatic choke?" Taylor said.

"Damn right. Impressive, huh?"

"How's it work? I hear those things stick."

"This one's been fine." When he pulled out into the traffic, he said, "Comfortable back there?"

"Yeah." The car was as luxurious as one of those hotels Bugsy Siegel was building out in Las Vegas.

"There's a cabinet under your seat," the driver said. "You want a drink, you got some whiskey in there."

"I'm okay."

The driver tipped his hat back. "If you need anything, just sing out. My name's Levinson."

"Where are we going?"

"Brooklyn. Williamsburg."

He swung the Cadillac onto the approach to the Williamsburg Bridge, a series of impossible curves that wound through the Lower East Side tenements. The buildings blocked the sun, so it was darker here, a little cooler. Traffic was always so heavy here that it caused the air to chronically reek of exhaust fumes. As they emerged into the sunlight on the bridge, the air smelled cleaner.

Taylor could see the Navy yards on the Brooklyn side of the East River. The yards weren't nearly as busy as they'd been when he'd first gotten back. The handful of ships docked there looked abandoned.

They drove through the narrow Williamsburg streets, coming to a stop at a large six story brownstone. The only available parking place on the block was in front of the house. Taylor suspected it was always open. Levinson pulled into it.

A group of boys played stickball in the street. Levinson watched the game as though he wished he were playing.

"We're here," he said, bounding around to open Taylor's door.

When Taylor knocked, a tall man wearing a linen suit opened the door. "You're Damon Taylor?"

"That's right."

"He's expecting you. Come in."

After he closed the door behind Taylor, the man in the linen suit frisked him quickly, efficiently. He did it without any explanation. Nor did he ask permission. He seemed to assume that Taylor would be expecting it.

"Follow me," he said,

He led the way to an elevator. Taking it to the third floor, he opened the door and they emerged into a large room. It ran the full length of the house, like a loft. The furniture groupings divided it informally into three parts. To his right was a lounge area, with a sofa, a coffee table and a couple of arm chairs. The center had been laid out as Leo Salmon's office, with a huge desk that gleamed from the wax that had been lovingly polished into it. A couple of leather chairs faced it. To Taylor's left was a library that the borough of Brooklyn would have killed for. It was huge, with floor to ceiling built-in bookcases loaded with volumes that actually looked as if they'd been read. A sliding ladder provided access to the upper shelves. Two overstuffed leather chairs, which matched the ones in front of the desk, with ottomans in front of them and glass topped tables next to them gave the area the atmosphere of a British gentlemen's club—at least, a version of the upper class club that appeared in one of P. G. Wodehouse's *Saturday Evening Post* stories.

A middle-aged man strolled over from the library and took a seat behind the desk. He was short, with a full head of gray hair, and he wore a tailored suit that was just a slightly deeper shade of gray than his hair, with a pale blue silk shirt and a red tie that had just a touch of a gray pattern in it. Taylor always wondered about men who wore suits and ties to when they worked at home.

"Mr. Taylor," he said, "please come in. I'm Leo Salmon." He waved to a chair opposite the desk. "Some coffee? Tea?"

"Coffee will be fine. Thanks."

"Joseph," he said to the man who'd led Taylor to the room, "We'll have coffee."

"Yes, sir."

"I've read your stuff, Mr. Taylor. You're a very good reporter."

"Thanks."

"Your magazine stuff is different from the material you used to do in your newspaper days, though. Tell me," he said, with a slight smile, "do you ever miss the old days on the *American*? I remember you doing some very interesting stories about life in this city."

"You remember them?"

"Well, to be honest, when I heard about your interest in me, I refreshed my reading, but, yes, I remembered them. I followed the stories when they were first printed. I especially liked your series on the gypsies. How did you gain access to them, anyway? I understand they can be quite secretive."

"I just hung around, kept showing up in places where they showed up. After a while, they began talking to me."

"The results were fascinating. Why did you go to *Crime Scene*?"

"Why not?"

"I'm not a diplomatic man, Mr. Taylor. You ask me why not, I'll tell you why not. The stuff you did for the papers made a difference to the quality of our daily life in this city. You explained the way we lived to us, showed us stuff we hadn't seen, even though it was right in front of us. You made us look at our everyday reality again." A quick smile flickered across his face and disappeared. "Your magazine work is crap. Well-written crap, but still crap."

"You may be right."

"Oh, I'm right. We both know that."

"You're right in that you aren't a diplomatic man."

"There's too many people around who will lie to you. You don't need another one."

"Why are you having me followed?"

Salmon held his hands out in a gesture of helplessness. "We have mutual interests. You can understand I had no intention of harming you, but I did want to know who you were talking to."

"I'm writing about a murder. When you say we have mutual interests, it doesn't fill me with confidence in my safety."

"Brownie Hobson's murder was as big a surprise to me as it was to you. I can assure you I had nothing to do with it. You have nothing to fear from me."

There were a lot more questions he wanted to ask, but he knew better than to push. When he'd first begun in this racket, he'd been as aggressive and pushy as any dumb, untrained cub reporter who had nothing but enthusiasm going for him. If a source didn't answer a question, he'd ask it fifteen more times, trying to beat the guy down. One of the first things Damon Runyon taught him was to take it easy. If your interview subject didn't want to answer the question, let it go, get him relaxed and, later on, ask the same question a different way. Keep coming back to it from different angles and, more likely than not, you'd find a way to ask it that disarmed the guy enough to make him want to answer it.

Joseph arrived with the coffee. It was delicious. No Horn and Hardart, no Automat stuff in this house. He nodded approval and Leo Salmon smiled.

"Glad you like it. I import it and sell it, mainly to restaurants and specialty shops. Back to the point, though. About *Crime Scene*? Your going to work there. Why?"

"Simple, really. I needed to do something different when I got back from overseas. Didn't want to go back to the same old thing."

"I can see how you must have felt. As I understand it, so many young men spent all those years just wanting to go back to things as they had been and when they got home they discovered that things had changed forever. They'd never be what they were again."

"It's not just that things changed. None of us were the same either. I got back, I found out the city was different and I was different. Didn't feel at home anymore. I mean, Christ, I was born here, lived in the city all my life and suddenly I'm feeling odd, a little weird, everywhere I go. It's like I'm looking at things I've seen all my life and I don't recognize them anymore."

He didn't know why he was telling Salmon this personal stuff, but then, he didn't know why he shouldn't be telling him. It didn't make any difference and that was the main thing different these days: nothing made any difference.

"I see," Salmon said. "That makes sense. Do you know how many people spend their lives searching for the one thing they can never have? All they want is for things to stay the same and that's the one thing that can't happen. Everything changes all the time. *Everybody* changes. Go through what you must have endured in the war and you can never be the same again, can you? How would you describe it? You lost your innocence?"

"You know, you're not quite what I expected."

"Because I'm intelligent, you mean?" He smiled like a man who was proud of his learning.

"Something like that."

"I'm not an educated man, Mr. Taylor. Like most people in my business, I was too poor to go to school. I never made it past the fifth grade. But I've found that schooling and learning are two different things. See that library over there?"

The bookshelves sagged under the weight of the books on them. They weren't neatly shelved. Books were stacked, piled, almost thrown randomly onto the shelves. Stacks of books and journals rested on the tables next to the reading chairs.

"That's where my learning comes from, Mr. Taylor. I fell in love with books and learning very early. It's not something I talk to my colleagues about, but one of my major regrets is that I never got to go to college. That room right over there became my university. Joseph helps, too. He's a university man and among his duties is tutoring me." He refilled his coffee from the silver service. "But we were talking about you needing a change. I imagine a factor in your going to *Crime Scene* was the chance to work with Lou Marsczyk?"

"He's one of the big reasons. Marsczyk's one of the greats."

"I know. Back in Chicago, he made life miserable for some people I know. There was not a lot of regret when he left town."

He added cream to his coffee and held the silver pourer out to Taylor, who shook his head. The coffee was too good to dilute with cream or sweeten with sugar.

"That's Lou, all right."

"If the facts are out there, he'll find them." Salmon hesitated a moment, watching the steam rise from his coffee. "And you're attending his finishing school."

Taylor didn't bother to answer.

"Let me ask you this, Mr. Taylor. You get around the city. You know something about everything that's goes on. What do you hear about an upcoming musical called *Finnegan's Rainbow?*"

By now he was getting used to a few things about Leo Salmon: the fact that the man loved language and grammar, as well as the sound of his own voice and the fact that he liked to skip from topic to topic. Taylor stayed relaxed. He'd get to what he needed in

Salmon's own good time.

"Well, for one thing, it's called *Finian's Rainbow*. Fact is, my upstairs neighbor is an actor and we were just talking about that show the other day. He tells me it's in trouble," he said. "It's undercapitalized and having trouble raising more money. It might not be able to open. People who know about these things, though, say if it does manage to open, it could be the biggest hit of the season."

"If it opens."

"Right."

"I've got an opportunity to invest in the show. I have to admit, it's an attractive proposition. Would you recommend I do so?"

As he allowed Salmon to pour him a fresh cup of coffee, Taylor had to remind himself that this man, charming as he was, charmingly ordered people killed.

"If you do, make sure you put in enough money to have some clout. If I were you, I'd demand a share of the partnership."

"They're in that much trouble?"

"Every bit."

"Why should I demand to be a partner?"

"As a casual investor, you won't see a penny until all the debt is paid, till it goes into profit. Even for a hit that can be a long way down the road. If they've got the right accountants, it can be never. As a partner, you'll get paid from dollar one. And you'll get a piece of the gross on all the ancillary income."

"Ancillary income. You mean the road shows, the film version, amateur productions, all that?"

"All the stuff that keeps money coming in for years."

"Don't regular investors get that?"

"They're supposed to. Sometimes it even happens. But their cut is based on net and it's tiny."

"I see what you mean. You know, the musical comedy is changing. It's becoming an art form again. *Oklahoma* changed everything."

Taylor shook his head. "I'm not a fan."

"You're an interesting man, Mr. Taylor. You've got a blind spot where the musical is concerned, but an interesting man nonetheless. Let's get down to business now. Why, precisely, did you want to see me?"

"I need to know what happened to Brownie Hobson and why."

"And you figure I can tell you?" Salmon raised his eyebrows. "Why?"

"He moonlighted doing muscle work for you. You've had people tailing me and you had a couple of guys beat me up. Call me a fool, but that kind of indicates to me that you've got a piece of this."

"Let me put my factotum on it." Salmon pressed a button on the intercom. "Joseph?"

"Yes, sir?" Joseph's voice sounded mechanical over the device.

"Mr. Taylor tells me that a couple of my associates beat him up. Find out if that's true. Immediately."

"Yes, sir."

"If it is, have those men come here."

"Yes, sir."

When he released the button, Salmon leaned forward and said, "I didn't have anybody work you over. That wasn't my doing. If anyone associated with me did that, he was working on his own." He hesitated, his brow raised as if he felt it important to indicate that he was thinking. "You know how unlikely it is that someone working for me would do something like that on his own initiative? That just doesn't happen. Joseph will find the truth of it before the day's over. I'll let you know what he finds out."

"If it wasn't you, who was it?"

"Well, now, that's the question, isn't it?" He poured another cup of coffee from the silver service. Taylor passed. "I can also tell you, I never directly hired Brownie Hobson to do anything. Again, if he worked for my organization, one of my associates, someone far down the line, hired him."

"They have that power?"

"I don't have either the time or the inclination to personally oversee everything. I decide policy, other people execute it. If they need to call in help, I have confidence they can do it right. At least, I had that confidence until this happened."

"Then if they weren't your people, a couple of those other people could have worked me over."

"Working over the star reporter for a major magazine is not a part of any sane policy. Even without knowing you personally, I could have predicted that violence would not cause you to back off. All it would do is make you more determined and that's exactly what happened, isn't it?"

"That's right," he said. "Why were you at his funeral?"

"Brownie's, you mean?"

"Exactly. If you had nothing to do with him, didn't hire him, why go to his funeral?"

Leo Salmon took a deep breath. "I'm going to require your discretion here, Mr. Taylor."

"Oh?"

"There's no need for anyone else to hear what I'm about to tell you." After a long pause, he said, "I didn't know Brownie. I did know his wife. I went to the funeral as a show of respect for her."

Small world, he thought. "You were sleeping with his wife?"

"No. She's a friend, that's all. I've known her all her life. Don't make it sound cheap. She's a very nice woman, Mr. Taylor. She deserves better than what she's getting out of life."

"You're right."

"You know her?"

"I talked to her. Seems like a nice woman."

"You're determined to find the truth about Brownie's death, aren't you?"

"You know how I hate not being able to finish a story?"

"To the best of my knowledge, the truth you're trying to find is not a threat to me."

"And if it was?"

He smiled again, but this time there was no warmth in it. "Then we'd be having a different type of discussion."

14

Joseph called at four that afternoon, while Taylor was putting together his story. "Mr. Taylor," he said, "Mr. Salmon asked me to call you. He wants me to assure you that no one working for him had anything to do with what happened to you."

"You sound kind of definite."

"I *am* definite. The investigation was thorough. You can have confidence in what Mr. Salmon is telling you."

"One hundred percent confidence?"

"Absolutely."

"Tell me this, Joseph…"

"What?"

"Give me one good reason why I should believe you."

"There's only one. Because it's the truth."

He cranked out another boilerplate story, a holding steady, marking the spot, nothing new to report story and it disgusted him. After he turned in his copy, he walked into Lou Marsczyk's office and threw himself into a chair, scowling. Marsczyk poured him a drink and slid it across the desk.

"You know what pisses me off?" Taylor tossed off some of the scotch.

"Bad whiskey?"

"I'm onto something. Somehow I've stumbled on to something important, something big enough that people beat me up to warn me off of it, and I haven't got any Goddamn idea what it is."

"Enough to drive you crazy, is it?"

"Damn right."

The sound of the crowd rose on TV and Marsczyk turned to see what was happening on the ball game. Ted Williams had hit one out.

Marsczyk shook his head in disgust. "You know, the thing about putting ball games on TV is you don't have to go to the Polo Grounds to find out how bad the Giants stink."

"Yeah."

"You'd think with Durocher managing them now, they'd be able to do something, but Christ, these guys leave a stench all over Manhattan. You go up there, you'll see this big parade. It's the crowd leaving the Polo Grounds to walk over to Yankee Stadium." He poured himself another drink. "So, what'd you pick up from Leo Salmon? That him on the phone?"

"Do you miss anything?"

"Try not to. That him?"

"His factotum."

"His what?"

"Secretary. Whatever you want to call him."

"What'd he have to say?"

Taylor watched the game for a moment. The picture on the screen was as shadowy and as snowy as last year's blizzard. He didn't care if Jerry Lester did have a show or how low Dagmar's necklines were, the fact was if the networks wanted to go anywhere with this TV thing, the technical quality of the picture was going to have to get better in a hurry. Otherwise, the medium was going to be a flash in a pan and people were going to go back to the movies, where the picture was big and clear.

"Salmon says he didn't have a damn thing to do with it. He didn't have me beaten up, didn't have anything to do with Hobson's killing, nothing. You know what his attitude toward all this is? It's all too unimportant for him to be bothered with."

"Another gang?"

"You think maybe we're making a mistake assuming a gang killed Hobson?"

"Like you said, two shooters, the Savoy, the sheer balls of the operation. It's all so public. There's got to be a reason for that. And the beating you took?" He poured himself another drink and held the bottle out to Taylor, who declined. "We got three families fighting it out for control of the city. Any chance Hobson got in the way of one of them?"

Taylor took a deep breath and said, "Fact is, I just don't know."

"Next week's another issue, another story. Why don't you go find out?"

He stood and headed for the door. "Well, seeing as how I don't have anything else to do."

When Walter Winchell glanced up and saw Sherman Billingsley leading Taylor over to his table, he dismissed the men sitting with him by waving them away as though they were flies. He pushed his hat backwards toward the peak of his scalp and leaned back in his chair, causing Billingsley to wince when he saw Winchell tilting toward the rear wall until the front feet of the chair left the floor. Taylor guessed the columnist could be rough on the fancy furniture.

Winchell could be rough on whatever the hell he wanted to because he knew Billingsley would accept it and just keep on smiling as though he were really happy about the way the columnist treated him.

"Damon," Winchell said, "glad you could join me." He signaled for his personal waiter. When he scurried over to the table, Winchell said, "Irish whiskey—Jameson's, isn't it, Damon?—for my friend, another bottle of champagne for me." He indicated the chair opposite him. "Sit down, sit down."

Winchell ignored Billingsley. Taylor figured he must be angry with the club owner again. These flare-ups happened all the time. Winchell would get all puffed up over some imaginary slight to his ego and refuse to speak to Billingsley until the club owner apologized. Then the columnist, in a big and always public display of compassion, forgave him and allowed things to go back to normal. But until he decided that the time was right for forgiveness, he'd sulk and threaten to take his patronage to some other club. He never did, though. Other clubs might expect him to pay his way.

"Good to see you, Walter," Taylor said.

"Same here."

Guy Lombardo was introducing Margaret Whiting, so Winchell signaled for him to be quiet. "I love the way this broad sings," he whispered.

They sat in silence while Whiting did her song. She was pretty good, Taylor thought, but he couldn't hear the magic that moved Winchell so much. When she finished and returned to her seat at the edge of the bandstand, Winchell applauded madly. The orchestra struck up "And the Angels Sing" and Winchell turned his attention back to Taylor.

"When it comes right down to it," he said, "Talent like that explains why I'm not a singer anymore. I just can't keep up with that. Never could."

Taylor waited. Winchell would explain why he'd sent for him in his own good time and there was no use hurrying him. He was proud of his sense of timing, a quality that he felt helped explain his radio success.

"So, exactly what have you been up to?" Winchell said.

"What do you mean?"

"You're making some pretty big enemies."

The dance floor was crowded. Taylor watched as the couples swirled around, executing their studied dance class moves. Unlike the Savoy, the house was filled with middle-aged women, dressed in elaborate evening gowns and with carefully styled hair and expensive jewelry that flashed and sparkled as they danced. These women were accompanied by their overweight, balding husbands in business suits.

"What kind of enemies are you talking about?"

"Every kind."

"Walter..."

Winchell held his hand out like a traffic cop to silence Taylor. "Just listen to me, young man. Take this as a warning from somebody who cares about you. You don't know what kind of trouble you're in." He stared at Taylor until the intensity of his gaze became uncomfortable. "All I can tell you is it's bigger than you can imagine."

"Exactly who's causing me this trouble, Walter?"

"Let me say this, Damon: get off of this story. It's the only way to get this trouble off your back."

"You're a reporter warning me off a story?"

"I'm a friend worried about your health. Your life might be in danger. No story's worth getting yourself killed."

"Who's going to kill me?"

Winchell's face took on a dramatic cast. He looked like a man imitating a statue. "All I can tell you is certain people are very upset with the direction your research is taking. I'm sworn to secrecy."

"Sworn to secrecy," Taylor repeated dully.

"You know I can't tell you who my sources are."

"Let me see if I understand this. You called me here to warn me that somebody's out to hurt me, maybe kill me. And you know who it is but you're not going to tell me because you can't reveal a source?"

He shook his head. "You make it sound so bad, Damon. It's not that I won't tell you, I can't."

"Walter..."

"Let me give you what I can, tell you what's going on." He held a hand out, a cop stopping traffic. "As best I can, that is. Brownie got mixed up in something bigger than he could handle. I'm not sure exactly what it was, but it's tied up in the garment industry wars. Well, I don't know exactly what happened, but Brownie somehow got in the way."

"That's what got him killed?"

It didn't fit. Leo Salmon had told him that the gangsters didn't have anything to do with the beating he'd taken. If Hobson's murder was connected to the gangs, then he was back to square one: who had beaten him up and why?

"Well, that's where it gets strange. You know Brownie beat up people who didn't pay their vig to the Gambino boys, didn't you?"

"He worked for the Gambinos?"

"Joe and Tommy didn't even know he was alive," Winchell said derisively. He was proud of his first name acquaintance with big-time gangsters. "Brownie was strictly small time. If somebody way down the line needed extra muscle for a particular job, he might throw a little work Brownie's way."

"So what got him killed?"

"You know that since Lepke got the chair, the garment industry's been up for grabs, don't you?"

"I'd heard something. We did a story on it but I didn't work it."

He tried to remember the details. Back in the twenties, Arnold Rothstein had descended on the garment industry like a plague of weevils on cotton. Rothstein, always needing money to support his gambling habit, specialized in playing both ends against the middle; designers paid him to keep out the unions, while the unions paid him to break down management so they could gain more power.

Rothstein had figured out early that prohibition wasn't going to last and gambling took his money as quickly as it came in, so he'd diversified, using the money his illegal casinos and loan sharking brought in to build an empire. He bought himself a platoon of politicians, judges and cops and moved into night clubs, more casinos, racehorses, blackmail, protection and drugs. If there was a buck in it, Rothstein was in it, too.

For a while he rode high, running just about every illegal activity in the city, but his compulsive gambling and his way of irritating the other crime families finally brought him down. In 1928, a couple of Louis Lepke's men shot him in the groin at the Park Central Hotel. He lingered in screaming agony in the hospital for two days before he finally gave it up and died.

With Rothstein out of the way, Louis Lepke and Jacob Shapiro took over the garment industry and operated it until Lepke trusted the wrong people and got himself executed back in 1944. Shapiro, who was muscle to Lepke's brains, couldn't hold onto it. For the past couple of years, all the families had been violating the deals they made to share the industry. One gang was going to take it over and all of them were fighting to make sure they would be the one.

"Hobson's death was connected to what's going on down there?" he said.

"Can't say for sure. When I pressed for details and, believe me, Damon, I did press, my sources reminded me that he also had a bunch of angry husbands after him. Brownie wasn't exactly monogamous, you know."

"His girl friend thinks he was."

"The one with the baby?"

"Yeah."

"That poor girl." He shook his head. "She deserves so much better."

"So you're telling me the Gambino family is threatening me?"

"I'm telling you that it could be guys associated with them. Not the top guys, hell, from what I hear they don't even know you're alive. But there are some people..." He let the sentence trail off. "Anyway, those guys are one of the things you have to watch out for."

"There's more?"

"And that's the part I can't tell you about." Winchell hesitated. He frowned, adjusted his hat a moment longer than was necessary and then said, "All I can tell you is this," he leaned forward, placed his palm beside his mouth and stage whispered, "Don't trust anybody. Don't trust anybody who's connected, don't trust the cops, don't trust a soul. You never know. All I can tell you is there are people who want you to stay away from this and they'll go to the Goddamn wall to drive you out."

"But you can't tell me who they are."

"Like I said, just go through the day figuring it's everybody."

He knew that was all he was going to get. "Thanks, Walter."

"You're not going to do a thing different because of what I told you, are you?"

"No."

"You're just going to keep on pushing, trying to get the whole story."

"That's right."

"Why? It's not that big a story."

Taylor shrugged. "Can't say, really. It just seems like the thing to do."

"I envy you that courage, Damon. You've got it, Runyon had it. Me, well, I just don't have that strength. I'm sorry, Damon. I wish I could tell you more. But, frankly…"

Taylor didn't want to hear anymore. If Winchell finished the sentence, Taylor would lose a man who might be one of the few friends he had. He knew the broadcaster had told him as much as he dared and he also knew that Winchell would not be able to face him again if he had to apologize for his own weakness.

"Thanks, Walter," he said quickly, rolling over Winchell's voice. "I appreciate what you did." He kept on babbling until he was sure Winchell wasn't going to say anything more. "You helped me a lot, gave me a direction. At least, I know where to look now."

As he left the club, Margaret Whiting was about to sing again. Let Winchell enjoy it. He needed something to pump him up after the way talking with Taylor had brought him down. So Winchell was a coward. Hell, he'd known that before tonight.

15

The next day, Taylor worked the phones until he couldn't take any more of the futility. Leaving the office, he took the subway uptown, heading for home. When he turned off of Broadway onto West 93rd Street, an old woman in a housecoat cornered him. She wore her hair pulled back and covered with a rag. Pointing to a dog turd on the sidewalk, she screamed at him in German. He held his hands out helplessly and walked past her toward his own stoop, as she continued to scream at his back.

The daily game of stickball was going on in the street. Pete Breshcher was at bat. He based his stance on Jackie Robinson's and, while waiting for the pitch, he circled the bat menacingly. The red Spalding ball came over the center of the plate, a perfect pitch and Brescher killed it, sending it sailing straight down the street, well over the head of Larry Kinsolving, the outfielder.

As Brescher circled the bases, Taylor called out, "Nice hit."

The kid waved back at him.

He was walking up the stairs before he realized that, in the middle of this small and everyday moment, this pleasant walk from the subway to his door, somebody could have shot him.

O'Bradovich answered his knock on the door with pieces of latex hanging from his cheeks. His nose had been widened and flattened and his right eye was swollen, almost closed. He must have been removing the makeup when Taylor knocked and the effect was grotesque. At this stage, with the material he'd used to pad his face dangling loosely, he looked like something out of The Phantom of the Opera. O'Bradovich stared at Taylor's face and said, "You still look like hell."

"You been checking yourself out in the mirror?"

"Hell, mine's makeup. It'll scrub off. Yours won't."

"Thanks. Come on up for a drink," he said.

"Love to. Give me fifteen minutes."

"I was working on a boxer, trying to figure out what a losing fighter would look like." O'Bradovich said. "You notice the eye? I based it on what yours looked like the other day."

"Why didn't you just use my face as a model?"

"Couldn't. Yours is clearing up now. Doesn't look half as bad as it did a couple of days ago. I needed something fresh. I wanted him as he was being helped out of the ring. So, you ever find out who beat you up?"

"Here's the deal," Taylor said, after he'd poured drinks for both of them. "It's beginning to look like either the cops or the F.B.I. did it."

"What?" O'Bradovich looked at him with disbelief.

Taylor was standing in front of the open window, watching the stickball game, his drink held loosely in his right hand. It crossed his mind that he made a good target here, but he refused to move, maybe out of some kind of stupid stubbornness. He would be damned if he was going to be backed down by threats passed on to him by somebody like Winchell. He scanned the street, though, checking to see if he could pick up somebody watching his place.

"Leo Salmon told me that gangsters didn't do it. He says nobody there's after me. Winchell tells me that I'm in big trouble. His sources say I better back off from this story. You know who Winchell's sources are?"

"He's got sources? I always figured he made that shit up."

"He's got sources. The cops and the F.B.I."

"Winchell's that close to the law?"

"He thinks he's a cop. He cultivates them, carries a bunch of honorary badges, praises the hell out of them in his column and on the radio. Let me tell you, man, nobody eats up flattery like a bureaucrat cop."

"But why would the cops beat you up?"

"They either think I know something or they think I'm going to find out something."

This news was too much for O'Bradovich. He stood, walked slowly across the room and stopped, his face screwed up. He began to speak, stopped, started again but then silently shook his head dramatically, as if he wanted to be seen clearly from the last row of the balcony.

"But that doesn't make any sense," O'Bradovich said. "If you knew anything, you'd tell it to the cops."

"If it was safe."

"What do you mean?"

He poured another drink. "What if a cop killed Brownie?"

"I don't know a hell of a lot about these things," O'Bradovich said slowly, "but it seems to me that if a cop did it, then all bets are off."

When he walked into the elevator at Vera Kelly's shop, Taylor saw that the operator who took him up was older than he was. The man had a defeated look about him. His shoulders slumped and his face was drawn and remote, as though he'd knocked back a couple of belts at lunchtime and didn't want anyone to know. Taylor figured him for a veteran having trouble making his way in civilian life again.

The man brought the elevator to a stop and slid the door open. "Fifth floor," he said.

"Thanks."

"Mr. Haynes' office is to the left."

The office door was open and the man who greeted him was as short and slim as a hand rolled cigarette. He dressed flamboyantly, in white linen pants that ballooned at the thigh and got progressively tighter down to the ankle, so that they looked like they belonged to a zoot suit whose owner was trying for good taste. His silk shirt looked like something Errol Flynn would wear in a pirate movie. He had a red bandanna tied around his throat.

"You must be Damon Taylor," he said. The hand he held out had a cigarette holder in it. No cigarette, just a holder.

Taylor shook hands awkwardly. "Thanks for seeing me."

"I'm Simon Haynes."

"You work for Vera Kelly, Mr. Haynes?"

Haynes stiffened his back, drawing himself up. He looked at Taylor with his lip curled, as though he'd just been insulted. It was a hard expression for him to pull off. He was too short and slight to make it work.

"I design for Miss Kelly," he said. "I do not work for her. Workers are people who sit at desks or sweep floors."

"She pays your salary?"

"Of course, but I'm not a simple employee. I'm a part of the creative team."

"I see. Sorry."

"That's quite all right. How can I help you?" He scanned Taylor like a doctor examining a sick child, clucking his tongue in disapproval. "My. You're quite the fashion disaster, aren't you, Mr. Taylor? The suit doesn't fit, it's the wrong color for you, and the tie, ugh. Some people can buy off the rack but you're not one of them. I can save you, though. If you just put yourself in my hands, I'll have you looking ten years younger and infinitely better."

"Maybe some other time. You know Brownie Hobson? The dancer?"

He shook his head and Taylor couldn't tell whether it was because he didn't know Hobson or was disappointed that Taylor wouldn't put himself in his hands. In some ways, the little man reminded him of Capote. Their voices were similar and they were both tiny. Capote, though, had a sort of magic about him, a sparkle in his personality that this man lacked.

"Can't say that I do," Haynes said.

"You don't know the man at all?"

"I don't believe so."

It was hot in this room. He could almost feel the heat rising toward the high ceilings. He unbuttoned his jacket but left it on so that the little designer wouldn't be terrified by the sight of his gun.

"You always design costumes for people you don't know?"

"I guess you caught me, Mr. Taylor. I told you a little lie, didn't I?" He fluttered a hand dismissively, as though wiping away the words he'd spoken earlier.

"I hope it's a little one."

"I knew Mr. Hobson and you're right, I did some work for him. You understand I wanted to keep it quiet because I did it under the table. Freelanced, you might say. If the firm had known I was doing it..." He shivered as though he'd remembered something incredibly erotic.

"You know he's dead."

"He was shot wearing my design, I understand."

"Bled all over your silk."

The office was a mess. Drawings, ranging from quick sketches to fully fleshed out color portraits, were piled on the desk as if tossed there like an open deck of cards. Material samples lay in heaps everywhere, in no apparent order. He didn't see how any work could be done in this office at all. He was used to disorder—he worked on a magazine, after all—but this place made Taylor feel jangly, ill at ease.

The huge floor to ceiling windows were dirty, so that the room had to be lit by overhead lamps, even though it was early in the afternoon. A large fan sat over in front of the closed window but it wasn't turned on.

"Excuse me, Mr. Taylor. I don't mean to make light of a tragedy. What can I do for you?"

"When was the last time you saw Hobson alive?"

He could feel the room getting hotter. There was a chance of rain today, the radio said. He hoped it would come soon.

"The last time I saw him? When he picked up his costumes."

"When was that?"

Up close, the little man looked older than he did at first glance. Taylor started in surprise; Haynes was wearing makeup. He watched as Haynes took out a pocket appointment book and opened it. Scanning the pages by running his finger down them, he stopped and held the finger in the air triumphantly.

"June 17," he said.

"Anything unusual about him that day?"

"I don't follow you. What do you mean?"

"What was his attitude? Remember, just a couple of days later, he got shot to death. Was he nervous about anything? Was he upset?"

"No, he was fine. He just came in, gave me my money, pushed the rack of costumes out the door and that's the last I saw of him."

Even as he told Taylor how calm Hobson had been, Haynes was shooting glances around, as if he feared the possibility of someone overhearing him. His hand shook almost imperceptibly. Taylor could read the tension in the man; it was as blatant as a comic book. He wondered why this guy was so terrified.

"Let me ask you one more question, Mr. Haynes?"

"Yes?" His voice rose a pitch and lost some of its volume.

"What are you so afraid of?"

He started. "What do you mean?"

"Come on, I can see it all over you. Something's got you terrified. What is it?"

Haynes took a deep breath. He took longer than was necessary to take a cigarette out of his pack of Philip Morrises, place it in the holder and light it. When he exhaled, he had control of his limbs again; his hand was no longer shaking.

"The only thing I'm scared of is that you're going to print this and cost me my job."

"But you're a part of the creative team."

"Look, you don't understand this business. There's only half a dozen major design houses and they've only got a couple of dozen slots open in them. And the truth of the matter is there's thousands of talented bright young men like me. There's not room enough for all of us in the industry. When you get a perch, you work hard, don't rock the boat and wait for somebody to notice how good you are. Eventually, good things can happen for you. Get noticed for the wrong thing and you're out on your ass. And the truth of the matter is, Mr. Taylor, when you get shoved out, you don't get back in."

"Maybe you shouldn't freelance on company time. I take it you used company materials? Company labor?"

"I was the labor. I did the cutting, the sewing, everything. Listen, Mr. Taylor, if you can just keep my name out of it..." He shivered again as though anticipating a slice of his favorite cheesecake.

Taylor closed his notebook and shoved it into his jacket pocket. "Relax, Haynes. You're not the story here."

The elevator operator seemed slightly happier on the way down. Closer to quitting time, Taylor figured. It was cooler on the street than it had been in the office. He crossed Fifth Avenue so he could walk back uptown in the shade. Since the two men who watched him come out of the building didn't follow him, he paid no attention to them. They looked like the last of the vaudeville acts; one was as short and tiny as Simon Haynes while the other looked as though he could block out the sun. The big one entered the building while the small one fell in half a block behind Taylor.

16

Frankie DeMarco's luck was changing. Since he'd decided to keep the group alive and take it over himself, he'd hit the streets looking for a little seed cash to put the Lindy Hoppers up on their feet again. He couldn't believe the rejection. It was like being dropped off a building. None of the people they'd made so much money for, the managers, agents, club owners, not a one of them was willing to put a cent in the pot.

And the dancers? Hell, they were making demands. They were ready to come back but not on the old terms. It was like they'd had a meeting or something and decided that now that Brownie was history, if there was going to be any more money coming in, they wanted a bigger share. The bastards wanted an even cut, which meant he was going to have to audition new dancers, which meant he had to have some damn money, which nobody wanted to give him. He hustled his ass off but still came home and gave his last few bucks to his bitch landlady, who wouldn't let him in the door if his rent wasn't up to date.

This morning, though, he'd gotten a phone call. Marty Lewis, the owner of the Brown Pelican, wanted to see him, said he had a deal for him. This was his chance. All these years, people had thought Brownie was the big man behind the Lindy Hoppers. Now they'd find out that it was Frankie all the time. It was Frankie's talent, his choreography, his *soul,* if you will, that made the Lindy Hoppers work. With the group reformed without Brownie in the lead, everybody would finally know the truth.

And the Lindy Hoppers were going to be a nationwide sensation because he had been in a bar the other night and had been struck not by an idea but a genuine inspiration, the sort of insight that makes you catch your breath and become lightheaded, almost like a man destined to become a saint receives a revelation.

Television.

It was happening, baby.

And so was he.

All he had to do was get Frankie DeMarco and his Lindy Hoppers on television and his fortune was made. There were four networks operating from four in the afternoon till after midnight and they all needed programming. Singers he'd never heard of were doing daily fifteen minute shows, and these variety reviews? Damn, the air waves were filled with them with more coming every day. Milton Berle had one that ran a full hour, *Broadway Open House* was starting up for two hours an episode and Eddie Sullivan was going on the air with his own hour, *Toast of the Town.*

They all needed a steady supply of acts.

They all needed him.

Which meant, of course, Frankie DeMarco was going to wind up with his own TV show.

All he needed was a little seed cash from Marty Lewis and he was on his way.

DeMarco pitched Lewis harder and stronger than he'd ever pitched anybody in his life, but the club owner didn't even bother to listen. Instead, he sat there, his fat ass hanging over the edge of his bar stool, his short little legs barely touching the brass rail, nursing a drink and checking his watch every once in a while. When DeCarlo began to tell him about the possibilities of television, he signaled for another drink and held his hand out like a traffic cop stopping the flow of cars.

"Frankie," he said, "there's only one thing wrong with your plan."

"What's that?"

"You're involved in it. Look, I didn't call you here to listen to you beg for money." His voice sounded like a gravel truck stuck in first gear. "Fact is, I'm here to do you a favor."

"But, Mr. Lewis, all I need is a few grand..."

"Oh, you need a hell of a lot more than a few grand."

"Well, fine, if you think so."

"Frankie, what you need is to find a way to keep your ass alive."

He wasn't expecting to hear this. He was stunned. "What?"

All you had to do was look at Lewis to know he hadn't been born with that name. As short as a fire plug, he looked like he'd have to be pushed through a doorway, that's how wide and round the man was. Wide as a truck. With his prematurely white hair and neatly trimmed beard, and his sharp suit, he had an air of sophistication around him, but you could still see the evidence of his immigrant parents just beneath the surface.

"You know, I'm taking a chance telling you this, but you and me, hell, man, I hate to see a guy go under 'cause he didn't know the score."

"What are you talking about?"

The club owner's fresh drink looked tiny in his huge hand. He took a sip, smiled approvingly and placed the glass back on the bar. All the time DeMarco had been sitting here Lewis hadn't offered him a drink.

"There's some people asking around about you. Word is they're the same guys that did Brownie."

"Why would they want me?"

Lewis raised his eyebrows. "Why'd they want Brownie?"

"Hell, I don't know."

"What I hear around, somebody thinks you do."

"Oh, Jesus. Mr. Lewis, who are these people exactly? Who's out to get me?"

"Come, on, DeMarco, even if I knew, it'd be putting my own life on the line to tell you. Just take it from me, these guys know what they're doing."

DeMarco found himself wondering how the weather was down in Miami Beach. Seemed like a good idea to go find out.

17

"Busy?" Taylor said.

Horace McCall almost forgot to take the cigar out of his mouth before he swigged from his coffee but caught himself in time. He dropped the cigar into an ash tray and took a drink of coffee before answering.

"Ever known me not to be?"

The noise level in the squad room was higher than usual. Detectives worked the phones, while others interviewed civilians or typed up reports. Even though McCall had a private office, the closed door didn't do a thing to keep the voices out. Through the window, Taylor could see Lucius Stander, a tall muscular detective, leaning threateningly over the man sitting next to his desk. The man cringed as Stander rolled up his sleeves.

"Got a problem. Thought maybe you could help me."

McCall looked at Taylor's face, his eyebrows raised. Finally, he said, "You look like hell."

"Should have seen me a few days back."

"Glad I didn't. Why didn't you call me when it happened?"

"Sure. You could've put your murder cases on hold while you turned all your manpower loose on finding a couple of goons who worked me over."

"I could've bought you a drink at least."

"You're right. I should have called you."

McCall's cigar had gone out. He took a box of wooden matches out of his desk drawer. The first match he used to try to get the cigar started again broke in half. He threw it angrily on the floor, struck another and relit the stogie, puffing furiously to get it started. It smelled like he was burning broom straw.

"Need some help, you said?"

"Two things you might be able to clear up for me. Why would the law want to work me over?"

"Maybe they heard you're going to vote for Truman," he said.

"I already thought of that. Can't help but believe it's not the reason."

"The law, huh? What level? Local, Federal, what?"

"I'm guessing either city cops or FBI."

"What makes you think it was them?"

"Winchell told me."

"Oh, well, hell, who can doubt it? I mean, if Winchell said it…"

"Okay, the man's an idiot, but he got more cops in his pocket than the mayor."

"And he says cops did it?"

"Or FBI guys."

"He said this?"

"Strong implication."

"What's their motives?"

"I was hoping you could tell me that."

McCall puffed on the cigar and discovered it had gone out again. He looked at it disgustedly, threw it in the trash can and took a pack of Old Golds out of his shirt pocket.

"You ever stop to think how much simpler your life would be if you just quit smoking?" Taylor asked.

"Shut up." He inhaled a freshly lit cigarette and smiled dreamily. "To answer your real question, I got no idea why the cops would work you over, except that you're obnoxious as hell, but, Christ, they've known that for years and let you slide. You're sure Winchell knows what he's talking about? I mean, if he does, well, that's a rarity right there, isn't it?"

"Leo Salmon tells me it wasn't mobsters."

"Leo Salmon. If anybody knows mobsters, it's him. You're talking to him now?"

"Mob guys were following me. I needed to know why."

"How'd you know they were his?"

"Logical guess. Brownie worked in clubs, Salmon's got the clubs tied up. Also he was at Brownie's funeral. The man's all over this thing, made sense it's him."

"What the hell are you working on, anyway?"

The Old Gold rested forgotten between his two fingers. When the trail of smoke rising from it entered his line of vision, he remembered the cigarette and took a drag. For a guy who smoked as much as McCall did, he didn't strike Taylor as being very good at it.

"Just the Brownie Hobson story. Got anything new on it?"

He shook his head. "Not a thing. How 'bout you?"

"You know anything about a guy named Simon Haynes? Works for Vera Kelly?"

"The designer?"

"Yeah. He designs for her. Also does some freelance stuff. He did Hobson's costumes. Under the table. When I asked him about Brownie, he got nervous. Very nervous, like there's something he's afraid of. Tried to tell me his nerves were just because he was doing under the table work, but I'm thinking it's more than that."

McCall stubbed out his cigarette, stood and walked stiffly to the door. Opening it, he called out, "Hey, O'Brien, get in here, bring the file on O'Dell Freeman."

"What's up?" Taylor said.

McCall pushed at the air, miming shoving Taylor away. "If you hang on, we'll only have to go through it once."

When a shadow fell over Simon Haynes' desk, he looked up from the sketch he was working on and saw Mickey Arrelano standing over him. Arrelano had a face as flat as an iron. A few days ago, when he'd dropped by for the first time, Haynes had been scared to death and not in that good way that he occasionally enjoyed. He'd asked around about the big guy and found out Mickey was one dangerous man. He'd done a lot of really bad things to a lot of people. The guys he talked to told Simon that Arrelano liked to hurt people and was very good at it. With Arrelano, it wasn't a game. He was serious about causing pain, didn't care who he beat up or under what circumstances, as long as he could make people hurt. All of this went through Haynes' mind in an instant.

"What do you want?" He asked. His voice broke in the middle of the question and he felt ashamed of his own cowardice.

"My friends tell me you been talking to that reporter."

"Your friends?"

"The people we all work for. They say you been talking to the wrong people."

"I didn't tell him anything. Really."

"Nothing?"

Despite his intention to sit still and face up to the man's questions, Haynes found himself standing and taking a couple of steps back. When his back touched the wall, he stopped, unable to figure out what to do, where to go. He noticed the odd little smile on Arrelano's face and wondered what it was that was amusing the man. Maybe it was just the possibility of causing Haynes some pain. A shiver coursed through him. Arrelano noticed it and his smile grew wider.

"Look, anything I told him would get me in as much trouble as you. I'm as deeply into this thing as you are. Jesus, I'm not crazy, Mickey. I don't want to go to jail."

Arrelano's voice sounded dreamy, faraway. "Did you just call me by my first name?"

"I'm sorry. I didn't mean it. It's just I'm afraid. I don't want to go to jail."

"Don't worry about it, Simon. You're not going to jail. The guys who sent me over here to see you want you to be clear on that. You ain't going to jail."

"Then you believe me?"

"A couple of guys called me this morning, asked me to do them a favor, so you can take it from me you ain't going to jail."

"What? A couple of guys? I don't understand you."

Arrelano crossed to the window. Studying it a moment, he found the lock, undid it and threw the window open. The sound of car traffic was deafening. Horns blew as though it were New Year's Eve. He leaned forward and stared down at the traffic jam five floors below.

"They ought to ban cars from this city, you know that?" he said.

Haynes frowned. Was he expected to answer that? He felt his face quiver, moving back and forth in quick, smooth movements. Arrelano stood with his back to him, watching the traffic. A crazy thought occurred to Haynes: all he had to do was race across the room and shove with all his might and Mickey Arrelano would go sailing out the window and fall to his death. The thought was powerful, but that was the problem with it. It was much more powerful than he was. He'd never be able to do it.

"Really," Arrelano said, "I was talking to a guy the other day, in a bar, you know, and he was telling me how private cars ought to be banned from Manhattan. Just buses and delivery trucks would be allowed in. And cop cars, of course. Made a lot of sense."

At this moment, Haynes only knew one thing for certain: he was in big trouble.

"Do you really believe me?" he asked again.

"Sure. You ain't going to say anything."

"That's right. I promised you before and I promise you again right now."

"Good. You promise."

Although his back was turned, Haynes could tell that Arrelano was still smiling. Again, he wondered what was funny. But when Mickey turned around, he saw the smile fade, to be replaced by a faraway but serious look as the scary man crossed the room toward him. When Arrelano reached the place where Haynes thought he would stop, he opened his mouth to speak but all that came out was a scream as the other man picked him up, carried him across the room and tossed him out the window as though he were a bag of garbage being dropped into an incinerator.

Wallace O'Brien shook hands with Damon Taylor, saying, "I've seen you around the station."

"Same here."

O'Brien was a light-skinned redheaded man with a scar over his right eyebrow. He wore the pants from a tan summer weight suit and a white shirt. His tie was undone, his collar open; his undershirt showed at his throat. Although he wasn't a big man, an air of menace emanated from him like the fragrance from cologne.

"You write for *Crime Scene*?"

"That's right."

"Beatings and robbings and killings for pleasure, all presented in like an evening's entertainment, right?"

"We hope it's a little more than that."

"Relax, O'Brien," McCall said, "we didn't bring the man here to give him a hard time."

O'Brien shrugged and said, "If it fits…"

"It's okay."

When they were seated around McCall's desk, the lieutenant held the file aloft and said, "O'Brien's working the O'Dell Freeman shooting."

Taylor shook his head.

"Freeman was the chief cutter at the Vera Kelly shop."

His level of interest increased. It was like discovering a complex word that had been driving you crazy in a crossword puzzle. A trace of a smile crossed his face.

"Vera Kelly?" he said. "He worked for her?"

"That's right."

"When he got shot, was he at the shop by any chance?"

"By every chance."

He could feel the excitement cause him to almost boil inside. The feeling grew; it was as if he were at the track and had intuited a winner, a horse he knew had to hit.

"When exactly did this Freeman person get it?" He asked the question even though he knew the answer already.

McCall flipped through the file. "June sixteenth."

"Bingo," Taylor said.

"Bingo?" O'Brien repeated. "We got a connection?"

"Brownie Hobson was at Vera Kelly's picking up his costumes on the sixteenth."

McCall picked up the phone and punched in an extension. "This is McCall," he said, "I want a comparison of the slugs that killed O'Dell Freeman and Brownie Hobson. Now." He listened for a moment and then said, "You know, I can't recall asking you if you were busy. What you got to figure is I don't give a damn if you're busy or not. The way I remember it, I said I want it now. You know what now means?" When he hung up the phone, he murmured, "Both men shot, who knows? Maybe we'll get lucky."

"Shooter use a .38 or a .32?"

"No," he drawled, "Freeman was shot to death by a BB gun. That's why I ordered a comparison." He flipped another Old Gold out of the pack. "Of course, it's a .38, you idiot."

"Okay, so it wasn't that bright a question. Still, it's going to be interesting if we get a match."

O'Brien said, "What's the connection between Hobson and Freeman?"

A knock came at the door. "Come in," McCall said.

Two detectives came in. They glanced around at the three men and the leader, a burly-looking guy in his fifties said, "This'll just take a minute. Lieutenant, we got a positive print on the gun."

"Refresh me," McCall said.

"The Seidman shooting yesterday? We found a gun dumped in the rain gutter. Checks out as the murder weapon and the husband's prints are on it."

"Bring him in. Ask him a few questions." McCall said.

"Okay." He nodded to the two detectives and they left the office.

"All right," McCall said, "the connection between Hobson and Freeman. That's the question. Right now, we don't have one. We've got to find it."

Taylor rubbed his chin with the palm of his right hand. "What if Hobson saw Freeman get it?"

"He's wandering around the Garment District at the wrong time?"

"Could be. Simon Haynes told me he came in, picked up his costumes and left, pushing them out on a cart."

"One of those carts they use to take clothes from building to building?" O'Brien asked.

"Yeah."

"Then he'd have to return it after he got the clothes in his car. He's all over Vera Kelly's."

"Why don't we find out what he saw while he was there? We got nowhere else to go." He glanced over at O'Brien. "Make sense to you?"

"Makes enough sense that I'm willing to take a couple of uniforms over there and ask a few questions." He turned to Taylor. "Anything turns up, I'll let you know."

Which meant that he didn't want him coming along. Taylor understood that. Most cops felt hampered by civilians and didn't want them around when they were working. Out in the streets, police work didn't always go by the book and the fewer people outside the force who witnessed them ripping pages out of the book and using them to start bonfires, the more satisfied the cops were.

"You'll call me if the bullets match?" he said to McCall.

"You'll be the third or fourth to know."

"I'll be in my office. Got the number?"

"Yeah."

There was nothing left to do but go back to the office and write up this week's story. It wasn't going to be much of a piece. Just a bunch of speculations, a what might have happened but we can't prove it story. He did get one break, though; while he was in the middle of his draft, McCall called.

"It's a match," McCall said. "Same .38."

"What about the .32?"

"Haven't found it yet. And you know something?"

"What's that?"

"I don't think it's going to turn up by your deadline."

At least he had a fact to work into his piece. Among all the rumors, ideas and guesses, it looked lonely as hell but, by God, it existed.

18

"This is delicious," Linda said. "Where did you find fresh rainbow trout in the city?"

"I know some people in the Fulton Fish Market. They take care of me."

He'd gotten to know them when he'd lived down there, back during what he still thought of as his *research the city* phase. When he'd landed his first newspaper job, Damon Runyon took him aside and said, "Kid, you ain't going to be worth a damn if you don't know every pothole in this town. What you got to do is get yourself a room in a boarding house in a different part of the city every few months. That way you can get out and learn the living hell out of the neighborhood, find out how it operates beneath the surface. When you got that neighborhood nailed, you move to the next one and do it all over again. That way you learn the heart of the city, one block at a time."

The advice made a lot of sense to him back then. It still did.

Still, he thought, if he'd learned the city that well, why did it all seem strange and different to him now? When he hit the streets, the buildings were the same, the subways and buses hadn't changed and the people still dressed and acted the way they had before he'd gone away, but they were as different as rocks from envelopes and he saw them all differently now.

Maybe the city claimed to be the same but it wasn't and he wasn't either.

She took another bite. "A man that knows where to find good fish and can cook it without drying it out to cardboard? You know how rare that is?"

"Thanks." Sometimes feeling rare wasn't a good thing.

He'd turned in his copy at two in the morning, picked up a cab outside the building and went down to the corner of Fulton and South Streets, where the day's business was just getting started at the fish market. Two huge market sheds with open fronts faced South Street and opened onto the unloading docks where the day's catch was being removed from the vessels tied up at the docks. In the old days, Taylor had always enjoyed coming down here. Now, he just stopped by when he wanted to pick up a few filets from his buddies at the Flag Fish Market. Before he went to bed, he slid a note under Linda's door inviting her to dinner that night. He hadn't seen her since they'd gone to the ball game, so he figured he had something to make up to her.

In the middle of dinner, the phone rang.

When he answered, McCall said, "I'm going to need you back down here."

"What's the problem?"

"Your boy Simon Haynes took a flier out his window."

"Say that again?"

"You heard me." He paused and then said, "You need me to send a car for you?"

Linda flashed him a quizzical glance. He winked at her, signaling her that everything was just fine, even though he knew it wasn't. McCall's offer to send a car wasn't a friendly gesture. It meant Taylor was probably in trouble. The real problem was that he didn't know why.

"No, I'll come down. You still in the office?"

"That's right." His voice sounded flat, like a telephone operator's.

"Give me half an hour." When he hung up, he said to Linda, "Stay here and enjoy dinner. I have to go back to work."

"What's going on?" She touched a napkin to her mouth.

All day, on her job, she wore her hair caught up in a tight bun. Whenever he ran into her in the building, her hair was as rigid as a public school, hidden under a hat. Tonight, it hung down, swirled around her face and she looked great. An unfamiliar twinge hit him and a feeling he hadn't experienced in a long time began to surface, but died as quickly as it had been born.

"There's been another murder."

"You can't even finish dinner?"

He debated taking the gun but decided, since he was going to the station house, maybe that wasn't a truly fine idea. He also didn't want Linda to see him handling the .45. She'd been really confused when she'd watched him dig it out of the closet; she hadn't enjoyed that and he didn't want to upset her again. He'd put her through enough.

"'Fraid not. You enjoy it, though."

"You're a great date. We went to the Savoy, somebody got shot and I went home in a cab. Time after that, you get the hell beat out of you at a ball game. This time you serve me dinner and somebody gets shot and you go running out the door."

"Can't help it. See you later."

"You're acting odd. This isn't just a reporting job, is it?"

"That's the thing, Linda, I don't really know what it is."

"You want me to come with you?"

"Thanks for the offer, but it won't do any good. I'll see you later."

"Give me a call when you get back. Let me know you're all right."

He frowned at that. It had been a long time since he'd checked in with anyone. Still, the idea didn't strike him as a bad one.

"Here's what we got," O'Brien said, eyes fixed on his notebook. "The elevator operator remembers taking you up to Haynes office a little after two and bringing you down about half an hour later. About the same time, a couple of dozen people down on 39th Street see Simon Haynes doing a swan dive out the fifth floor window and do a perfect landing on top of a delivery truck." He took in Taylor with a sweep of his eyes. "Guess how many guys used the elevator during that time."

"Not a whole lot, I'm guessing."

"Just you. You're the only guy who went up the elevator or came down. Since Haynes' office was five pretty steep sets of stairs, it's pretty safe to assume that nobody walked up. That leaves you."

"Actually, it's not at all safe to assume nobody used the stairs," Taylor said. "I'm a murderer, I don't want anybody to see me, do I?"

"Nobody else went up there."

"What you mean is nobody else took the elevator up there. What are you telling me here? You think I tossed him out the window?"

"I'm thinking you're the only guy there. You had opportunity and means."

"How about motive?"

"You tell me. Why'd you do it?"

Turning to McCall, Taylor said, "Your boy's lost his mind, Lieutenant. You know damn well I didn't do Haynes in."

"Right now," McCall said, "The only thing I know is I support my detectives. Other than that, I don't know anything."

"Why the hell would I do that to Haynes? I never even met the man till yesterday afternoon."

"All we got's your word for that," O'Brien said.

"I love it when a man wants to clear a case, but let's see if we can keep it sane, okay?"

McCall sat stonily behind his desk, a cigarette in his hand, an empty coffee cup on the desktop. The smoke curled from his cigarette and he appeared to be fascinated by it, but Taylor knew his attention was focused on the two men in front of him. His silence was louder than O'Brien's voice.

"Maybe you'll tell us why you'd do it," O'Brien said. "Maybe you're lying about not knowing him."

"O'Brien, you realize of course that after I left Haynes, I came here. What you're suggesting is I head over to Vera Kelly's place, kill a man I've never met before and then drop by the precinct, have a cup of coffee with the lieutenant here and tell him I just got through talking to Haynes. That makes sense even to you?"

O'Brien put his notebook back in his pocket. His pale skin was flushed, causing it to look splotchy. His scar looked white and stark, like one of O'Bradovich's makeup effects. He sat down, stretched his legs out and let the silence linger in the air like pollen, waiting for the tension to build up in Taylor.

"Here's what I know," he said finally, "we got two murders down at the shop and another one connected to it...."

"You don't think Haynes was maybe a suicide?"

"Doesn't make sense. One guy goes down in the place, maybe he takes himself out, but when it happens to three people that are linked to each other? The pattern doesn't suggest suicide."

"Wait a minute. All you've got is a bullet connecting Freeman and Hobson. Sure, Haynes made the guy's costumes, but that doesn't mean they're all three partners in crime. It's kind of a big logical leap, isn't it?"

"The connection's sound, Taylor. Don't go blowing smoke at me."

"Hold on a second," McCall said.

O'Brien shot him a look.

"Taylor, you said the guy was nervous, acted like he was scared of something?"

"Yeah."

"Scared enough of somebody or something to lose control and do himself in?"

Taylor thought for a moment and then shook his head. "No, O'Brien's right about that part of it. I can't buy suicide. It's too big a stretch. He was scared, yes, and he was definitely scared of somebody in particular, but he wasn't that far out of control. Somebody tossed him."

"You should know," O'Brien said.

Taylor took a deep breath. Despite himself, his hands were shaking and he shoved them into his pockets, noticing that McCall had observed the movement—the man didn't miss a move. Even though he hadn't done anything, even though it didn't make a damn bit of sense to think he had killed Simon Haynes, he was becoming as nervous as a wolf with his paw in a trap.

"Horace," he said, "you don't believe I did this. You know I didn't. Why the hell would I throw a guy out a window and then come waltzing down here and tell you I was there?"

"He's got a point," McCall said to O'Brien.

"He can't establish an alibi so he's trying to cover his tracks."

"Pretty weak," McCall said, with a shake of his head.

"Leave me alone with him for five minutes and I'll get the Goddamn truth out of him."

"I'm thinking maybe that's not a very good idea," McCall said. "Working over the top reporter for the biggest crime magazine in the country doesn't strike me as a very smart thing to do." Turning to Taylor, he said, "Like I told you, I support my detectives. O'Brien wants to talk to you, I let him bring you in. He wants to try to build a case on you, I'll go with him till it becomes obvious he's out of line. Right now, O'Brien likes you for this thing and he's got a couple of reasons. Not enough to work you over, but he's maybe on the trail of something. If he finds what he's looking for, I'll turn his ass loose on you. Got it?"

"I got it."

"'less something breaks to clear you, consider yourself a suspect." He tried to blow a smoke ring. The attempt was as big a failure as the League of Nations. "You got any ideas on this?"

"Let's take it step by step," Taylor said. "We got a guy doing work under the table. We got his customer, who goes in to pick up his goods. There's a killing the day he does this and next thing we know these two get killed."

"Conclusion?"

"Only two ways to look at this. One, these three are up to something they shouldn't be, or, two, they saw something they shouldn't have."

"What this suggests to me, O'Brien, is you need to investigate both possibilities," McCall said, "Find out just what the hell's going on down there."

"We just let this bastard walk?"

"He'll be around. Won't you, Taylor?"

Taylor turned his hands out and shrugged helplessly. "I got nowhere to go."

19

When Taylor got home, he found Truman Capote leaning back on his couch, legs extended and crossed at the ankles, his head lolling on the top of the back support, smoking a cigarette. His hair, usually so carefully combed, looked as though Linda had been rubbing his head like a puppy's. Linda sat across the room from him, looking at him as though she were a herpetologist who had just discovered a new breed of snake.

"It's painfully slow work," he was saying to Linda, "I go over each story a dozen times, at least. There are passages that I've worked over for months, trying to get them right."

"Well, let me tell you," Linda responded, "it's worth the effort, the stories are great."

"Ah, Damon," he called out when he noticed Taylor in the doorway, "why haven't you introduced me to this wonderful, bright, insightful woman? She's read my stories."

"Great."

"That's more than I can say for you." Capote placed a new cigarette in his holder. "And we're supposed to be friends."

"How are you, Truman?"

"Fine. I was in the neighborhood doing an interview, so I thought, well, naturally, I have to stop and see my good friend, Damon. And surprise! This beautiful creature was here all by herself."

"I had to go out."

The smile Capote flashed a smile at Linda was bright enough to light up a broom closet and about as sincere as a politician up for reelection. "You went out and left this creature by herself? Whatever is the matter with you?"

Taylor crossed to the kitchen and poured himself a drink. Holding up the bottle in an offer to the others, he waited until they turned him down and then added ice cubes to his own glass. An almost crushing tiredness crept over him and he found himself sighing like an old man about to climb the stairs of a tenement. He just wished that Capote and Linda would both go home so that he could sleep.

"Horace McCall wanted me downtown," he said. "Seems like Simon Haynes got himself killed this afternoon. Right after I left him."

"Vera Kelly's designer?" Capote said.

"You knew him?"

"I've got some friends who work in fashion. I met Haynes at a couple of parties. So, somebody killed him?"

"Threw him out a fifth floor window."

Capote shivered and leaned forward, the lazy attitude gone now. He was focused, energized, ready for something. Taylor could almost see him thinking.

"Who'd want to do something like that?" Linda said.

"The Louis Lepke mob, probably." Capote said.

"What are you talking about?" Taylor said.

"Gather round." Capote waved his arms wide. "I'll tell you a story." Flashing Taylor a smile, he added, "You'll want to take notes."

Taylor took a seat opposite Capote. Placing his drink on the table, he took out his notebook and a pencil. Capote smiled again; he was enjoying this.

"You remember Lepke, don't you, Damon?" Capote asked.

"They executed him while I was in Europe."

"1944. You know he had roast chicken and shoestring potatoes for his last meal?"

Taylor and Linda looked at Capote as though he had suddenly started speaking in tongues. He noticed the way they were looking at him and shrugged.

"I find details fascinating, don't you?" he said. "Anyway, Damon, you're going to know some of this, you probably reported parts of the story, but it's all brand new to Linda here, and you need some context for where it's all going to lead, so bear with me, all right?"

"Sure."

"Well, all right, then. We go back to the twenties. Louis Lepke—his real name was Buchalter, you know—anyway back in the twenties, he was working for Arnold Rothstein. He was an ambitious boy and he saw that the bootlegging business was getting overcrowded. He needed another specialty. Damon, what did he choose?"

"Labor racketeering."

"I knew you knew part of the story. You're right. He went after the unions. Now, at that time, Little Augie Orgen had the unions sewed up. Louis served an apprenticeship under Augie. When he figured he had the business learned, he killed Augie and took over."

"He just murdered him?" Linda's voice was disbelieving.

"As easily as you'd stub out a cigarette. Linda, that's how you rise up the career ladder in the big time crime business," Capote explained.

"How do you know all this?" Linda said.

"Like I told Damon a while back, I just find crime fascinating. I've made quite a study of it. Anyway, he took over the business and refined it. Augie had specialized in strike-breaking, he provided goons to beat up union guys. Lepke began selling his services to both sides. He worked for both the strikers and the strike breakers. Then he just took over the unions. Tom Dewey, the next president of the United States..."

"You think he's going to win?" Linda said.

"Oh, it's already done. Truman hasn't got a chance. Not that I like it, you know. I'm afraid of what he's going to do when he takes office," Capote answered.

"Why are we talking about Dewey?" Taylor said.

"Oh," Capote answered, "because he called Lepke the worst industrial racketeer in America. And he played a big part in Lepke's downfall. When Dewey was the special prosecutor going after the gangs, Dutch Shultz wanted to have him hit. Lepke thought killing Dewey would bring down more pressure than they could handle, so he arranged to have Schultz hit instead. Now, you don't go killing somebody as big as Dutch Schultz without drawing a little attention. After Schultz got it, the Feds began taking a closer look at Lepke and they indicted him on labor racketeering and drug charges. He went underground, went into hiding and the feds launched a nationwide manhunt for him."

Capote was having the time of his life. All of the attention in the room was focused on him and he loved it. He paused now, lit a cigarette dramatically, exhaled deeply and flicked his ashes into the tray before he continued.

"To get things back to normal, Lucky Luciano tricked him into surrendering."

"Wait a minute. Wasn't Luciano in prison?" Linda said.

"Good girl." Capote praised her as though she were an A student. "He was but it didn't make any difference. If you can't run an outfit from prison, you don't deserve to be a crime lord. Anyway, Luciano put out the word that he'd arranged a fix. All Lepke had to do was turn himself in and he'd get off scot free. By the way, why do they say scot free? Turns out it refers to the Scandinavian word for taxes, skat. The British turned it into scot. So it means getting away with not paying your taxes...."

"Truman, the story?" Taylor prompted.

"Haven't you always wondered about that? No? Oh, well. To get back to the point, this is where Walter Winchell comes in," Capote said, nodding to Taylor. "Winchell walked Lepke down to the FBI office and surrendered him to J. Edgar himself...."

"The man who says there is no organized crime," Taylor said.

"Exactly. That's the man, all right. Anyway, Lepke got a big surprise. The feds sentenced him to fifteen years, Dewey added another thirty-nine for racketeering and then he began taking a look at the Murder Incorporated activities." Turning to Linda, he said, "Did I tell you he also ran Murder Incorporated?"

"Thomas Dewey ran Murder, Incorporated?" Linda looked incredulous.

"No, silly. Lepke did."

"Oh, well, that makes more sense."

Taylor wondered if she were kidding around, making fun at Capote's expense and found himself hoping that she was. He was afraid, though, that she wasn't.

"Anyway," she said, "No, you never told me about that."

"Maybe," Taylor said, "that's because until tonight he had no idea you existed."

"That could explain it," Capote said. "The fact is, though, Lepke did run Murder Incorporated and every once in a while, just to keep his hand in, he did a killing himself. Dewey got him for murdering a candy store owner in the Bronx and they sentenced him to the chair. They fried him in 1944. And you know the rest of the story?"

"No," Linda said, "I don't know the rest of the story. Tell me."

"What's Lepke's execution have to do with Simon Haynes?" Taylor said.

"Simple. Since Lepke's death, the garment industry has been up for grabs. All of the families want it."

"Why?" Linda said.

"It's a gold mine. You got the truckers' unions, and if you can't skim millions from them, you're not really trying. Then you get into ownership of the houses themselves. See, it's a cash intensive business. Design houses always need to raise a lot of cash in a hurry, especially during the fall and spring seasons. The mobs lend them the money and get them to place a guy or two on their payroll. To look after their money, you understand. Pretty soon, the designers have partners they never counted on."

"You figure that's what happened at Vera Kelly?"

"I think if I were you, that's the direction I'd be going in."

Taylor poured a fresh drink. This time Capote joined him.

"Look," Taylor said, "If I'm one of the families trying to take over a design house, I'm going to have to take out the guys the other families have already got in there. I don't see Haynes being any mob plant."

"How do you know?"

"He didn't strike me as a mob type."

"Why not?"

Taylor hesitated. He wasn't ready for this conversation. Capote didn't make it any easier for him. The little man's smile was small and sly, as if he knew something no one else did and wanted them to know about his secret knowledge.

"You're trying not to tell me that he was a homosexual?" Capote said.

"Well..."

"It's hardly necessary, but thanks for the attempt at discretion." Capote lit a cigarette, going through the same elaborate procedure as before. "If he wasn't a plant from one family or another, then the question becomes what did he see that he wasn't supposed to?"

"Or what did he learn about some other way."

"Right. Any ideas?"

"Nothing at all."

"So what do we do now?"

"We?"

"I told you, I want to cover crime."

"Come on, Truman, *PM*'s never going to let you write about this."

"They will, if I get a good story."

"Unless the victims are Negroes or Jewish, crime doesn't get covered in *PM*. You know that."

"Then I'll freelance it somewhere. You've got to let me be a part of it."

"Come on, Damon," Linda said. "You know you need the help."

"You also have to consider," Capote said, "that I've got a solid block of knowledge you need. Not to mention that I know people in the design houses. I can get you into places you can't get near."

"We'll see."

"Fine. What do we do first?"

"Find out if anybody's going after the Vera Kelly shop."

"Or if anybody already has it."

20

Mickey Arrelano reviewed what he knew about Mannie Francesca. Mannie's was a name he'd heard all his life and one of the few he'd ever respected. When he'd been a kid running the streets, he and his friends had told Mannie Francesca stories the way some kids told tales about their dads. Whenever something outrageous, something you couldn't imagine happening—a hit in a restaurant or barber shop, a daring daylight robbery—they chalked it up to Mannie. The man was a legend. Back during prohibition, Dutch Schultz and Legs Diamond had been at war. Schultz tried to hit Diamond a thousand times. On three separate occasions his men had blown so many holes in Diamond, he'd have leaked a glass of water, but Diamond had pulled through each time and wiped out a dozen or so of Schultz's guys for payback.

Mannie had seen an opportunity and in 1931 he'd taken Diamond out and gotten him good and drunk and then, along with two of Diamond's men, took him home in a cab. Half dragging the man, he'd helped him upstairs to bed, left him sleeping like a baby and, along with Diamond's boys, had taken the cab back downtown. With his alibi established to the satisfaction of the Diamond gang, he went back uptown, walked into Diamond's apartment and shot the sleeping man three times in the face.

The next morning, he went to see Dutch Schultz and told him what he'd done. Schultz had offered him a job on the spot. Think of it, Mickey told himself, the guy had hit a man as a job interview. That took balls.

Now, with Schultz dead and gone, Mannie was a big man in Frank Costello's family and was heading up the takeover of the fashion industry. And since he figured if that audition tactic had worked for Mannie, it might work for him, he'd hijacked a garment truck as an audition.

And when he'd gotten the phone call asking him to take out that design fag, he knew who'd placed it, even if the guy hadn't identified himself.

So now, having been called in for an interview, he stood in front of Mannie's desk, his hands in front of him, clutching his hat by the rim. As he stared at the man behind the desk, he toyed with the rim of his hat. A huge man stood to his left, a couple of paces behind him and Mickey was afraid that if he said something wrong, the big guy would crush him like a grape.

Not that Mannie himself was a walk in the country. Mannie was as intimidating as the electric chair.

"What is it exactly you want?" Mannie Francesca said. He sounded bored.

Arrelano thought Mannie looked ill at ease in a gray flannel suit, as if he'd put it on to have his picture taken and wasn't at all used to it. The collar was too tight and his tie had an unpracticed knot that caused it to cast to the right side, as though blown by the breeze. Mickey had on slacks and a shirt, with the shirt tail outside his pants. He thought maybe not getting dressed up had been a mistake.

"What do you mean?" he said.

"You hijack a truck and bring it here to me. Nobody told you to do it. So, tell me, what are you up to? What do you want?"

"Look, Mr. Francesca, I don't want nothing in particular." Since Francesca hadn't brought up the hit on the design fag, he figured he'd better not mention it either. "It's just I was in a position to do you a favor, so I thought I'd go ahead and do it."

Francesca smiled at the huge man who stood behind Mickey. "Joey, he's doing me a favor. For nothing."

"Ain't that nice of him?" Joey said. His voice was deep, but soft and the lack of volume caused it to be more frightening than if he'd screamed.

"If you want to keep on my good side, kid, one thing you will not do is come in here and bullshit me. Nobody does nothing for nothing."

Francesca's voice had somehow coiled like a snake, so that Mickey, who wasn't afraid of anything, found himself just a touch on the nervous side. Suddenly aware of the way he was playing with his hat, he forced himself to stop.

"Okay," Mickey said, "What I hear is you're going after the trucker's union. I figure maybe you need a soldier, a good man with some initiative, a go-ahead straight-up guy who can get things done."

"And you're that man?"

"Yes, sir. I am."

Francesca tapped his desktop with his fingertips, creating a rhythmic noise that sounded to Mickey a little bit like a Gene Krupa solo. The big man behind him, Joey, he remembered, hadn't moved. Mickey could hear his breathing.

"Let's say you got a point. Let's say we're reaching a point where a few more guys in the field won't hurt. Maybe you can explain to me why, out of all the guys in New York, I need you." Francesca didn't bother to look at him.

"You haven't heard of me?" Mickey was shocked.

"Why the hell would I have heard of you?"

This wasn't going the way he wanted it to. The room was suddenly cold and Mickey knew he shouldn't have said what he had. It made him sound like he was trying to be a big man and, Christ, there wasn't any bigger man than Mannie Francesca and here Mickey was, trying to make an impression and not doing it at all. If he was making any impression at all, he was causing the guy to dislike him.

"I been around. I done some stuff." Jesus, why had he said that? He was making things worse and worse. Right now, he could smell is own nervousness.

The man behind the desk looked disgusted. From behind him, Joey said, "Want me to tap him, boss?"

"Not yet." Looking at Mickey, his eyes oily, he said, "Okay, you're pretty fucking impressed with yourself. You still ain't shown me why I ought to be impressed with you. I keep looking at you but you ain't showing me nothing."

"Fact is, Mr. Francesca, I'm good. I ain't scared of anything..."

"Not even Joey back there?"

"Well, maybe him. Anybody with a brain's going to be a little bit scared of him. But I'll tell you this. I'm good and I follow orders. You tell me to jump him and beat the hell out of him, I'm all over him. I might get my ass kicked, but I'm all over him."

"That a fact? You follow orders?"

"From a man I respect? Without asking the first damn question."

"You know, there might be one more favor you can do for me."

He'd said, "one more favor," instead of a favor. So he knew that Mickey had already done something for him. There it was, an indication that Francesca recognized that he'd taken out the design fag for him.

"Yeah? What's that? Just tell me what you need."

"There's a reporter, a guy from *Crime Scene* magazine. You ever read it?"

Mickey frowned and shook his head. "I, well, I don't do much reading."

"Figured. The guy's name is Damon Taylor. He's beginning to be a nuisance, he bothers me a little. It would be nice if he was out of my hair." He gave Mickey that look again. "You understand what I'm saying here?"

"Oh, sure, but why?"

"That's a question."

"What?"

"You said you'd do what I said without question and the first damn thing you do is ask a question."

Mickey scowled and shook his head rapidly. "It don't make no difference why. I'm on the job. Damon Taylor, you said. Consider it done."

"I'll be grateful." Turning to the huge guy, he said, "Joey, we got something untraceable he can use?"

Joey waddled out of the room, returning a moment later with a .38 Smith and Wesson Police Special dangling from his fingers. He handed it to Mickey, who dropped it into his coat pocket.

When he got outside, Mickey was amazed to find he'd completely crushed his hat.

21

Janie Hobson sat beneath the el tracks, about twenty feet from the steps leading up to the train, eating an ice cream cone. When she saw Taylor approaching, she frowned. The street was crowded with mothers gathered in small circles chatting as their children played in the street.

As he walked over to Janie Hobson, Taylor noticed a few unemployed men gathered under the street light, drinking beer out of paper cups. Two of them still had the short, close cropped haircuts the military had given them; he figured them for veterans having a hard time getting started again. The city was full of them.

"Mrs. Hobson?"

"You back again, Mr. Taylor?"

"Call me Damon. If you don't mind, I've got a few more questions."

"I don't know what I can tell you that I didn't tell you before."

"Mrs. Hobson..."

"Please, I haven't been Mrs. Hobson for a long time. You want me to call you Damon, you call me Janie."

She licked ice cream off of her fingers. The act struck him as somehow sensual. Since he'd been here before, Janie Hobson had been taking better care of herself. Her hair had been styled and it looked as if she'd had a touch of color added. She was also paying more attention to the way she dressed. Before, she acted as if she didn't give a damn. Now she did.

"How are you getting along?"

"Pretty good," she said. "I've got a job now. I'm a secretary up in the fish market. It's hard work and I don't make a whole lot of money, but it could lead to something."

"Good for you," he said. "Janie, I've been finding out some weird stuff about your ex-husband. Maybe you can help me. Did you know he ran with mob guys?"

"I knew he knew them. He was one of those guys who took a kind of perverse pride in knowing gangsters. He thought it gave him some kind of status. I figured he just met them in the clubs we worked."

"Do you know who he was close to?"

She finished her ice cream cone. "Oh, for God's sake, he was so silly. He'd get all pumped up, thrust his chest out, and act like he knew a bunch of secret stuff that nobody else had any idea of. He liked to pretend he had big secrets, so he didn't tell me anything. That would be betraying the boys, he said."

"What are the odds he really did know something?"

"Oh, come now, Mr. Taylor..."

"Damon, remember?"

"Sure. Anyway, you knew Brownie. Would you trust him with anything important? The man was an idiot, a buffoon." She lit a cigarette. "And I'm an idiot for ever marrying him."

"Why'd you marry him, anyway?"

"I was young and I was stupid. What you've got to realize is that even back then, he was all puffed up with plans and schemes." She looked up at him. "When you're young and you figure you can't stand one more night in your parent's apartment and somebody exciting comes along, you tend to lose your good sense." She tried a smile but it didn't quite come off. "By the time you figure out you made a mistake as big as the Chrysler Building, it's too late."

"Don't be so hard on yourself."

She stood suddenly, so quickly that he lost focus and blinked. "Come on, Damon. You want to talk about that son of a bitch, you're going to have to buy me a drink."

The Lion's Den Tavern was a shot and a beer kind of place—small, with a scarred bar that had the names and initials of regulars carved into it, along the right side of the place. A few rickety tables were scattered on the sawdust floor and a jukebox centered the back of the room, a restroom door on each side of it.

They sat at the table nearest the jukebox and since the only other customer, an old drunk who looked like he spent most of his waking hours in here, had glared at them and staggered out as they came in, they were the only drinkers in the place. Janie Hobson tossed off a large swallow of her cocktail and sighed.

"I didn't used to do this," she said. "It used to be I hardly drank at all. I mean, I'd watch Brownie toss the stuff down until he threw up on his suit coat and I thought it was the most disgusting thing in the world. Look at me now, though. Sitting in here in the middle of the afternoon, cadging drinks off of you."

"Take it easy, Janie."

She stared at her drink. Even though she kept her face averted, he could tell from the slight racking of her shoulders that she was crying. He felt he ought to touch her, but held back; he didn't know her that well. She could misinterpret the gesture.

"I won't be able to do this much longer, though. I've got a job now. Did I tell you?"

"Yeah, you did."

"It's not dancing or acting, but it pays the bills. And, believe me, as soon as the alimony ended, there were plenty of bills. I tell you how much he left me in his will?"

"Not a whole lot, I'm guessing, considering you had to get a job."

"Nothing, Damon. Not a damn penny. He died flat broke." She looked up at him and quickly away, cutting her eyes to the right, so that he wouldn't see her tear up. When she had herself pulled together, she still refused to meet his eyes, focusing on the drink and said, "Thing you have to understand, Damon, is the pure fact of the matter is Brownie was a son of a bitch. He didn't do a damn thing but party all the time. He ran around on me and finally, when he knocked up another woman he left me." She tossed off her drink and signaled the bartender with her glass. "So, here's the deal. Since he was such a total bastard, how come I still have mixed up feelings for him?"

"Sometimes you can't control who you love, you know? Falling in love happens despite your best judgment."

"I'll tell you one thing for sure," she said, with a sad shake of her head. "I'm not sure love has anything to do with it. I don't know what this feeling is. All I know is I don't want it."

When her new drink arrived, she took a swallow and tried to smile again. The expression was there, he could see it, but there was no force in it. Too many conflicting emotions were running through her.

"One time, he surprised me." She laughed bitterly. "Hell, he was always surprising me, but this time it was good. Without even telling me, he went up to Carey's limousine service—you know, up at Grand Central?—and rented a car so we could drive down to Virginia Beach. We spent two weeks there, staying in a cabin right on the beach, swimming and boating all day and making love all night. It doesn't embarrass you when I talk like that, does it?"

"No, it's fine."

"Anyway, we did it all night and half the day every day and, you know something, he opened up and talked to me. Told me all kinds of stuff that was really important to him, about his dreams and ambitions and fears and, damn it, I fell in love with him all over again." She raised her eyebrows in an expression of helplessness. "We hadn't been home two weeks before he started running around on me again."

"I'm sorry."

"Did he have to make me love him all over again before he pulled that shit? Don't you think that was unfair?"

There was nothing he could say to that and he didn't want to sit here all afternoon while she got drunk and fell into a depression as deep as a well. If he could have helped her, that would have been one thing, but he could tell she didn't want any help, not right now. All she wanted was to wallow in it for a while. Taylor figured it was time to change the subject.

"Look, what could he have known that might have doing that got him killed?"

"How would I know? He left me, remember?"

"You didn't have any contact with him after he left?"

"None."

"You've got no idea why he got himself killed?"

"I know exactly why he was killed. Because he was one rotten son of a bitch."

Lou Marsczyk walked back to where Taylor waited, carefully working his way around the jammed together tables—the tiny club was becoming popular, so the managers tried to ram in as many people as possible. He carried a drink in each hand and, placing one in front of Taylor, he said, "Here you go."

"Thanks."

"You ever been here before?"

They were in the Famous Door, one of the dozens of jazz clubs that had sprung up on 52nd Street between Fifth and Sixth Avenues. The block was so crowded with clubs that people called it Swing Street. The jazz scene had erupted in this neighborhood like a volcano.

When the first entrepreneur had discovered there was a couple of bucks to be made in a small and intimate midtown jazz club, he converted the lower floor of a 52nd Street brownstone into a space that resembled a nightclub and before he could even frame the first dollar he made, jazz guys all over the city had flocked here to the street. Within a few weeks, Club Downbeat, Jimmy Ryan's, the Three Deuces, the Onyx, the Spotlight and half a dozen others were up and running.

You could walk into any one of them, stand at the bar and nurse a beer while you listened to some of the best musicians in the country. Then, you could walk across the street to the next club and do the same thing. Over the course of an evening, you could hit them all. Two bucks would get you a night of the best jazz America had to offer.

Taylor had been down here the night before last, catching up with Joe Turner at the Onyx. When he was singing for listeners instead of dancers, Joe's show was entirely different, much more jazzy and soulful, right at home in one of these listening clubs that were designed to showcase the new music the city's musicians were developing.

None of this had been here when he'd gone to war. Back then, the block had been a quiet residential neighborhood. Now, it had been taken over by Bohemians, guys and girls all dressed in black, carrying notebooks and mimeographed pamphlets of modern poetry, the street people who used to haunt the coffee bars around Bleecker and McDougal. Every night, as soon as it got dark, they emerged like vampires from their coffins and took the trains uptown. When the clubs closed at dawn, they made their way back to the village. The Bohemians—and the music, of course—brought the tourists, those from out of town and from the outer boroughs, and now the clubs were packed every night.

Tonight, Dizzy Gillespie, a trumpet player who'd made his name with the big bands up in Harlem, had brought in a quintet to play the music he was crazy about, an up to date, modern, frenetic jazz that was based on African and Cuban rhythms. Taylor hadn't had a chance to see him play but had heard he was good—O'Bradovich raved about the band—so when he needed a session with Marsczyk, he'd suggested they come here. They'd arrived early so they could grab a table and now, with the dinner dishes cleared, it was covered with Taylor's notes.

He brought Marsczyk up to date, letting him know where he was on the story and when he was finished, Marsczyk just sat there silently, rubbing his chin with his thumb and forefinger.

When he spoke, his voice was quiet and the words came slowly, almost as though he were bored with them before he even articulated them. "So what you got here is the biggest Goddamn mess you can imagine."

"Funny, that's what I was thinking."

He glanced over at the bar. Dizzy Gillespie stood there, propping a foot on the rail, his elbows on the bar. He was sipping a draft. The trumpet player wore a dark suit. Until you caught sight of his brown beret and his goatee, you could have mistaken him for a bank clerk.

"Let me try to focus it by summing it up for you," Marsczyk said. "Brownie Hobson gets those silly little costumes of his made under the table at a fashion house that's being taken over by the mob. Being an unlucky soul, he strolls in there to pick up his uniforms and walks into the middle of three crime families fighting it out for control of the whole fucking business. Taking a guess, I'm betting he sees a murder."

"Sounds good, but we can't be sure of that. Not yet."

"Nope, but it's the best guess. Brownie sees a design guy, maybe a guy that ain't cooperating with one of the families get it. So the question becomes..."

"I know. Why doesn't he run?"

"That's right. The guy just goes back to his normal life, dancing in public, spending all his time in clubs owned by gangsters or, at the very least, frequented by gangsters every damn night of the week. For a guy who witnessed a gang hit, that doesn't make a damn bit of sense."

"Unless he's tight with one of the families and thinks he's got a get out of jail free card."

"And it turns out he ain't as tight as he thinks he is?"

Taylor sipped his drink. "Problem is, we can't prove any of this."

"Maybe not," Marsczyk admitted, "but it's a scenario that pulls all the elements together, makes the whole thing make a little bit of sense, at least. And you can use it to explain why he goes back to his old life instead of taking off."

Gillespie's drummer, a wiry guy with huge biceps and skin the color of coffee, was setting up his kit over on the stage. Taylor could tell he was eavesdropping, overhearing every word they were saying. The musician's interest was piqued; he wanted to hear more.

"Brownie knows the shooter, is friends with him maybe," Taylor said. "He figures he's safe."

"Right. But if that's the case, how come he got himself popped?"

"Because, if you believe the people I've been talking to, Brownie's an idiot. He's an idiot with a big mouth, loves to talk about how important he is, how many big-time gangsters he knows, all the inside stuff he's privy to."

"You figure Brownie talked himself to death?"

"Could be, but what I really figure is the shooter didn't wait to find out if Brownie's going to blow off or not. He knows he's dealing with a big mouth, a pest and that sooner or later he's going to be bragging, dropping hints about knowing some big secrets or something. I'm betting somebody figured why wait to see whether he runs his mouth off or not? He's a detail, that's all. An *i* they forgot to dot."

"So somebody decided to go ahead and dot the *i*?"

"In a really public way, so that if Brownie *had* said anything, the people he'd talked to would know better than to repeat it."

"So, at this point, all we need's a little proof."

As he tightened the rim of his snare, the drummer's eyes met Taylor's and he raised his eyebrows and shook his head slowly. Taylor grinned. The drummer shrugged. They had a silent conversation for a moment until Taylor noticed someone at the bar.

He froze for a moment, feeling the muscles in his neck tense. Then, sighing as if what he was about to do didn't really please him, he stood up.

"Excuse me a minute, will you?"

The tall man at the bar with his back to the room sensed movement behind him as Taylor approached and turned just in time for Taylor's fist to smash into his face. The impact drove him back against the bar and Taylor hit him two more times. As the man tried to reach into his coat, Taylor slammed him in the stomach, driving the upper part of the man's body forward. Reaching into the tall man's coat, Taylor grabbed the gun the guy had been trying to pull out. As someone else jammed a gun into his ribs, he shoved his into the tall man's stomach.

"Back off," he said to the man who held the gun to his ribs, "or I'll blow this bastard's guts out."

"Put it down or I'll kill you."

"Not before I kill your buddy here."

"Ain't neither one of you going to kill anybody," Marsczyk said as he broke a whiskey bottle over the gunman's head. The man fell like a chopped tree.

"Damon," Marsczyk said, plucking the gun out of the fallen man's hand, "what the hell are you doing?"

"These are the sons of bitches that worked me over at the ball game."

The tall man wiped the blood from his lip. "I'm about to reach into my jacket," he said. "I'm getting my ID. Nothing else." He pulled out a shield in a leather case. Flashing it, he said, "I'm FBI, you dumb son of a bitch."

Dizzy Gillespie stroked his goatee and said, "Jesus Christ, how I'm supposed to compete with a show like this?"

22

"My name's Warren Brogan," the tall man said. He spoke as though he expected them to recognize it. "This is Special agent Tony Brigati."

Brogan's lip was split and a bruise was forming on his cheek. He took a seat behind his desk, placing a hand at each end of the green felt desk protector, resting his palms as if he were about to push himself to a standing position. He glared at Taylor and Marsczyk as though he wanted to intimidate them, like a cop beginning an interrogation. Brigati stood over in the corner, rubbing his head, content to let his partner take the lead. There were no personal items on the desk—no family photos, no note paper or pens. It was as impersonal as a subway stop. Taylor wondered if it was really Brogan's office.

They were in the FBI headquarters in the Federal Building down near Courthouse Square. Taylor had been in the building a couple of times before but had never penetrated this far into the recesses. He knew he was on the fifth floor but the agents had led them so deeply into the labyrinthine depths on the floor, he wondered if, had they told him to leave, he'd even be able to find his way out. He figured that was part of their strategy, to keep him off-balance.

"I'm figuring you know who we are," he said.

"Oh, yes," Brogan said. "Fact is, Taylor, you're becoming quite a, oh, I don't know, not a problem exactly, but certainly an irritant. I don't know why I don't just lock your ass up."

"Probably because you're up to something you shouldn't be touching."

"What the hell are you talking about?"

"Come on, Brogan, taking me into the bathroom at Ebbets Field and beating me up? Warning me off a story? The Bureau doesn't operate like that. You guys like to haul us down to the Federal Building, show us the full force of the feds and try to intimidate us. You don't use fists. What's going on? You up to something J. Edgar wouldn't like?"

Lou Marsczyk drew a flask from his coat pocket and took a drink. After he wiped his mouth, he grinned. Taylor wondered what he thought was so funny.

"You shut up, Taylor."

"Maybe if you told me what's going on," Taylor said, "we can find a way to do something about it."

"I know exactly what we're going to do about it. You're going to get the hell off this story."

"I don't suppose you're familiar with the phrase 'fat fucking chance?'"

Brogan fingered the bruise on his cheek. "Don't push your luck, Taylor."

"Look, Brogan, you don't really think you're going to just tell me to get the hell off a story and I'm going to just say 'fine' and walk away, do you? It doesn't work like that."

"Then maybe if I throw your ass in jail."

"Will you just stop it with the empty threats? You're not going to throw me in jail. You do and *Crime Scene* will have a hundred reporters on your ass in an hour. You'll be the story of the century."

"You wouldn't do that," he said to Marsczyk.

"I'd love to. I'm thinking I just might do it anyway, just for the sheer fun of it."

"How 'bout if the two of you disappear."

Marsczyk took another drink. "You know, I can see a couple of thing wrong with that idea," he said. "First off, all those reporters we were talking about? They'll be out looking for us and writing up every single detail they find out. And they're very good. Might take 'em a while but they'll find us. And every week they look is another national story. Second, you're not going to kill us, so sooner or later you got to let us surface and when you do, we'll walk out with the story of the fucking century. Third, my staff knows we're in the building right now. I don't go anywhere without one of my people following. She saw you bring us here. Matter of fact, she followed us in a cab and is sitting outside the building right now. We don't come out, she alerts the magazine and its lawyers and you drop into a sinkhole you'll never be able to crawl out of."

"You'd do that to your country?"

"Sure, if my country was acting like a jackass, like you are," Marsczyk said. "I love you federal guys, every time you don't get your way, you start babbling about the fate of the nation, like whatever you're up to is a fucking national security problem." He inhaled. "So why don't you just stop the bluffing and tell us what the fuck's going on?"

Brogan frowned and then glanced over at Brigati, who nodded almost imperceptibly. You'd have to be observing very closely, as Taylor was, to notice it. He'd just gotten an insight into the balance of power between the two agents.

"All right. Taylor, you walked right into the middle of an FBI investigation."

"And?"

He slammed his fist on the desk. "Goddamn it, I tell you you're fucking up a federal investigation and all you can say is 'and?'"

"Yeah, that's pretty much it. Especially since I got no idea what kind of investigation it is, whether it's even legitimate or not."

"Matter of fact," Marszcyk added, "We don't even know this *investigation*," he bit the word as if it were sour, "is really happening. All we've got is a bunch of vague words from you and, let's be realistic here, so far your reputation for honesty and openness is about as attractive as a sack of shit."

Leaping to his feet, Brogan leaned forward, his fists clenched. His teeth were clenched and when he spoke, he sounded as if steam were going to shoot out of his ears; he reminded Taylor of Elmer Fudd in a Bugs Bunny cartoon.

Maybe he'd take in a movie tomorrow evening, after work. Take Linda, maybe. She could use a night out; the last time he'd seen her, she'd looked tired and draggy, as if she'd been working too hard. She was a huge Clark Gable fan and he'd heard that Gable's new one didn't leave any lingering stench behind in the theater.

Take in a comedy. No, maybe a drama. Tonight was comedy enough for anybody.

"All right," Brigati spoke for the first time. Standing, he walked over to the desk, shoved his hands in his pockets and said, "We're building a case against Tommy Lucchese, spent the best part of two years on it and you," he pointed at Taylor, "come waltzing right into the Goddamn middle of it. I'm standing watching three years of hard work going down the tubes because of you, Taylor. And I don't like it. Not one Goddamn bit."

"Why are you so hot on Lucchese all of a sudden?" Marsczyk said.

"He's been a mob chief for, what, close to twenty years now?"

"Tommy's family is one of the gangs trying to sew up the Garment District," Taylor said.

"I couldn't care less about the damn Garment District," Brigati said. "Fact of the matter is, he's got half the Goddamn cops in this city in his pocket."

"As well as half the elected officials," Brogan added. "He's got Thomas Murphy on his payroll..."

"The police commissioner?" Marsczyk asked. He took out a notebook and a pen.

"You mind not taking notes?" Brigati said. "You know who introduced him to Murphy? Armand Chankalian. You know who he is, of course."

"The assistant DA."

"That's right. Look, the man's pockets are deeper than hell. When he was looking to become a citizen, his good friend Congressman Louis Cappozzoli greased about a hundred wheels for him."

Brigati let the silence build the implications of what he was saying. Taylor let it all sink in, chewed it over and when he spoke, his voice was soft:

"There's only one way he could build a chain of influence like that and keep it going. He's got to have the mayor, too."

"Back when he was just starting to build his base, Lucchese met Murphy. He cultivated him like a movie agent trying to land a star. See, Tommy's a bright guy. He figured out early that he could have these guys after his ass or he could have them as allies."

"And allies were better," Brogan added.

Marsczyk said, "He learned that from Tony Accardo, back in Chicago. While Capone was getting all the publicity, Accardo was the guy running the town. One time he and his wife took a vacation to Europe. Their good friends, Mr. and Mrs. Tony De Grazia went along with them. De Grazia was a lieutenant, thirty-seven years, on the Chicago police department."

"Look," Taylor said, "you can talk about going after Lucchese all you want to, but Lucchese doesn't move without checking in with Frank Costello." He hesitated, waiting for the FBI man to answer. When he didn't, he continued, "And Accardo. Accardo's in business with Frank Costello. Nothing happens in this town, hell, man, very little happens across the nation, without Costello saying so."

"That's a very sensitive topic."

"Yeah, because J. Edgar is in love with Costello," Marzyck said.

"I wouldn't put it that way."

"No? He has dinner with Frank when he's in town. Frank calls him every day with tips on the horses. Because of Frank, J. Edgar claims there is no organized crime in this country. Fact is, he's in his pocket and if you think he's going to let you go after Costello, you're as crazy as he is."

"You leave the director to me."

"Come on, man, you know who you're dealing with here," Taylor said. "Costello's got more politicians and judges in his pocket than the president. He's been cultivating them like Goddamn garden flowers since he took power and he's responsible for most of them being in office. Hell, he's even got the mayor..." He stopped. Frozen by the expression on Brigati's face. Reading the agent's face as though it were the cover story in *Crime Scene*, he understood. "You're after the mayor. You want to bring down O'Dwyer."

"Among others, yes," Brigati said slowly. "This town needs cleaning up, Taylor. And we're going to do it."

"Yeah, you and Wyatt fucking Earp."

Brigati ignored him. "We're going to do it and you're going to have to get out of the way. Every step you make is right into the middle of our investigation. Your buddy, Leo Salmon? He owns more politicians than he does books." When Taylor looked at him quizzically, he said, "Sure, we've seen the library. What you've got to figure is that when Costello wants a public official or a high ranking cop bought, Salmon is the one that makes it happen."

"So, you're out to bring down Costello, Salmon, Lucchese and their little group of politicians and cops..."

"It's not that little," Brigati said. "And, yes, we're out to bring it down and, yes, you're in the way. What do you propose we do about that?"

"I still don't see exactly why I'm in the way."

"Because you're poking into the Garment District and Lucchese's busy as a beaver wrapping up the industry."

"You're saying Tommy's got something to do with Brownie Hobson's killing?"

"We're not saying anything," Brogan said.

"Quiet down, Frank," Brigati said. "Look, Mr. Taylor, I don't know who killed Hobson. If I knew, I'd let you in on it just to get you out of my hair. I'm supposing—and this is just supposition, mind you—that his death is connected with something he learned that concerned Vera Kelly, which, you may or may not know, is now completely owned by Tommy Lucchese."

"It is?"

"Tommy's been lending them money for a couple of years now. They missed a few payments." He shrugged. "Anyway, if you start stirring things up... No, that's wrong, you're already stirring things up. So, Tommy's going to be on his guard and if he is he might just find out how close we are to him." He smiled. "Oh, another thing. It appears that he's getting tired of you. Your termination has been discussed."

"That happens on every story. Look, you say he might find out how close you are to him. You ever figure that if he's got all the cops and half the DA's office on his pad, he already knows?"

He shook his head. "We're way too careful for that."

"I hope so. You know how easy it would be to underestimate Tommy. And how dangerous."

"You might want to keep that fact in mind yourself, Mr. Taylor."

When Taylor and Marsczyk came out into the night, Mickey Arrelano watched from a doorway across the street. What the hell was Taylor doing in the Federal Building this time of night, he wondered, and what was going on when he and his buddy beat the hell out of a couple of guys in a jazz joint and then went downtown in a cab with them? And who was the broad in the other cab, the one they were getting into now?

His assignment was getting more complicated. Maybe he'd better watch this guy for a couple of days before he popped his balloon. At the very least, he'd better call the man and tell him what he'd seen tonight, see what he thought. There was an all night drug store over on Broadway with a pay phone in it, so he hurried over there.

He knew the pay phone was there because maybe ten years back, Legs Diamond had been making a call in it when Mickey shot him full of holes. Diamond had lived and Mickey would never be able to figure out how. He'd been one hard as hell man to kill but Mannie Francesca had finally gotten the job done, which impressed the hell out of Mickey because good men had been trying ever since Diamond first got out of line and they just couldn't pull it off. Francesca had succeeded where everybody else, including Mickey, had failed. That was one reason, a very big reason, he wanted to work for Francesca. Mickey admired the man. If he spent enough time around him, some of the man's magic might rub off.

23

"The two guys Taylor and Marsczyk beat up in the bar were FBI agents." Mannie Francesca spoke slowly, patiently, as if explaining a complicated math theory to a slow high school student. "They been trying to put together a case against the boss."

Mickey drew away as though the telephone was warming up in his hand. "No shit," he said, "How do you know?"

"Come on, Mickey, wouldn't I be piss-poor criminal if I didn't know? It's my job to know these things."

"Well, then, why are they messing around with these reporter guys?"

Francesca grew very quiet, saying nothing, but Mickey could still hear his breathing. That confused Mickey. What the hell kind of way was this to be on the telephone? He wondered what he was supposed to do and decided the best thing to do was just wait.

After a long pause, Francesca said, "I'm not going to tell you that, Mickey."

"You ain't?"

"No. I want you to think about it and explain it to me."

"You do?"

"Mickey, you want a job in my organization. My people can figure things out. You want to be one of them, you got to be able to figure things out, too."

"So this is like a test, huh?"

"Exactly."

"You want me to think."

"You got it."

This was hard for Mickey. For him, thinking was always connected to direct action, like saying to himself, "I think I'll kick that guy's teeth in," before he jumped him. To just think and not do anything afterward was strange. It was the kind of thing that had driven him out of school.

He screwed his face up as if the act of thinking required muscular effort and for a moment everything was blank as a cloudy night but then a spot of brightness appeared.

"The FBI guys think those reporter guys are going to get in the way," he blurted.

"Very good, Mickey, but there's still a couple of questions. Why do they think they're going to get in the way and what do you think we ought to do about it?"

Mickey thought he was fixed for good this time, but then he realized that even thinking he was fixed was a thought that didn't lead to hitting anybody or anything. He relaxed and saw that once the bright spot appeared, it grew larger and brighter, lighting up all of the sky in his mind.

"It's got something to do with that dancer that Taylor's writing about," he said. "Somehow that dancer's connected to the boss and they figure if he writes the story, it's going to ruin their case."

"Mickey, I salute you. Now, the last question: what do you think we ought to do about it?"

This one was easy. "You want I should pop their balloons?"

"Mickey, Mickey, Mickey."

Francesca spoke slowly as if the words pained him and Arrelano could hear the disappointment in his voice. Damn it, count on him to get the easy one wrong. He frantically shook his head back and forth, trying to get it to work right, trying to get a light on where he'd gone wrong. He could see the light in there dimming.

"It's not what I want that counts," Francesca's voice was calm again. He'd gone once more into his patient teacher mode. "It's what *you* think. It's the decision *you* make that's important."

"Oh, well, I think I ought to just blow their asses off."

"Then, if that's your decision, why don't you go ahead and do it?"

"You got it."

"It's important to do it right."

"The gun you gave me. I guess I ought to get rid of it after I do the job?"

"Now you're thinking, Mickey."

True, the picture didn't stink but it didn't exactly create the fragrance of roses either. Gable played a big time advertising man with no scruples who was assigned by Sidney Greenstreet, his boss with even fewer scruples, to land Deborah Kerr for a big radio ad campaign. Kerr, of course, is way too pure to play those kinds of games and Gable, of course, falls in love with her and you could see every single scene unfold about five minutes before it appeared on the screen. The picture was as predictable as snow in winter and while it was supposed to be shocking, while you were supposed to be repulsed by the lack of ethics in the ad game, anybody who'd ever turned on the radio, watched a TV set, read a paper or a magazine knew more than the film makers, so the response was a yawning "who cares? What you got to show me that I don't already know?"

Linda loved it, though. Get Clark Gable and Deborah Kerr on the same screen and it wouldn't make any difference if they washed cars for two hours, she was in heaven.

"How 'bout a drink?" Taylor said, as they left the theater.

She turned down Broadway and he followed. "Great. Downtown or neighborhood?"

"Up to you."

"You know where I haven't been lately? Toots Shor's."

"I swear to God," he said, "I don't know why you like that place."

She shivered, smiling. "It's so *masculine*. All those boxers and baseball players and gamblers..."

He laughed. When they reached the middle of the block, the crowd thinned and he stepped toward the curb to hail a cab. As he raised his hand, out of the corner of his eye, he saw a little guy step out of the alley. The man's hand was in his jacket pocket and the look on his face was one Taylor had seen before; he'd seen it every day for four years in the war and had hoped he'd never see it again. It was the face of a man who'd made a decision that he was going to kill and as soon as he saw the look, Taylor did what the war had taught him to do; he pulled his weapon and fired.

The first bullet hit Mickey Arrelano in the chest and an expression of disbelief appeared on his face as he still tried to raise his own pistol, the safe one that Francesca had given him. The expression deepened when the second bullet hit a couple of inches beneath where the first one had penetrated and try as he may he just couldn't raise his gun and when the third one slammed into his chest, he glanced down at the hole and then up at Taylor as if saying well, Christ, you did it that time.

He fell to the ground and one of Mickey Arrelano's last thoughts was that he'd been set up, that Francesca hadn't given a damn whether he got the reporter or the reporter got him. Somehow

Francesca won either way. His very last thought was phrased as a question: where the hell did a damn reporter, a guy that sat at a typewriter all day, for Christ's sake, learn to shoot like that?

24

McCall looked at his stub of a cigar in disgust and tossed it in the wastebasket. Picking up a pack of Old Golds, he lit one and tossed the pack back on the desk. After he exhaled, he looked at the cigarette as if he suspected it contained an illicit drug. After he examined the pack one more time, he turned his attention to Taylor.

"You know who the guy you killed was?"

"All I know is he's a guy with a gun coming after me."

"His name was Mickey Arrelano. He'd been in and out of jail all his life. Assaults, burglaries, attempted murders, suspect in half a dozen killings we couldn't pin on him. One of your genuine bad guys."

"I'm not surprised."

"Oh?"

"He came out of that alley ready to kill me and anybody that got between me and him. I couldn't let that happen. Hell, he might have hit Linda here."

Linda drew nearer to him and shuddered. "Oh, my God," she said, "it all happened so fast that till you said that just now, it never crossed my mind I might have been shot myself."

He put an arm around her. "It's okay." To McCall, he said, "Am I in trouble?"

"A couple of dozen witnesses all said it happened just like you described it. Unless you managed to paper Broadway with shills, you're off the hook. 'Course, there is a little matter of a war souvenir you ain't got a license to carry, but I don't see much happening on that account." He picked up a report from his desk. "One thing you'll be interested in. Soon as I saw Arrelano was carrying a .38, I had myself a little hunch, so I had it checked out. It's the same gun that did Brownie and that guy in the design house."

"That a fact?"

"One of those true facts. You took a double murderer off the streets and got yourself one hell of a story. Good night's work for you, huh?"

Taylor didn't answer. It was around one in the morning now and the heat had broken. A breeze strong enough to rustle the papers on

McCall's desk drifted through the open window. It felt good. Outside he could see a night shift detective writing up a report with a suspect handcuffed to his desk. Otherwise the squad room was quiet.

"There's still the shooter with the .32."

"What are you," McCall said, "a perfectionist? I clear a case for you and you ain't satisfied. We got Mickey and what you got to figure is we might not ever find his accomplice. Since you got through with him, he sure as hell ain't going to tell us who it was."

"And you're willing to be satisfied with what you got?"

"You know me better than that, Taylor. I got to tell you, I'm grateful to have something, anything. Nice to see the pressure lifted, you know?"

After they left the precinct house, they took a cab back uptown and stopped off at Billy Flynn's bar. Linda was tense, almost shaking. Her eyes darted around and she worked at her highball as though it were medicine. Linda took a big swallow of her highball. Taylor could tell one wasn't going to do it for her tonight.

Billy Flynn's was a neighborhood bar on 8th Avenue that didn't pay very much attention to the closing laws. A couple of drunks stood in front of the jukebox, shoving in nickels and punching up songs. Right now, the jukebox was playing "I Can't Be Satisfied," a new song by a Chicago bluesman that Joe Turner was raving about who called himself Muddy Waters. Taylor liked its rawness, its primitive pulse; you'd never hear it on the "Make-Believe Ballroom."

Linda downed her drink. "Look, Damon, I know this is important to you, but I just don't want to talk about it, all right?"

"I understand."

She rubbed her arms, raising her shoulders as though she were cold. The room was warm, though, so Taylor knew what she was thinking. He ought to say something, he thought, there should be some magic set of words he could use to relax her, make her feel better, but there weren't any.

"I'd appreciate it if you'd just see me home."

He stood. "Sure."

They walked back to the building in silence. When they arrived, Linda ascended the stoop, stopped at the door as if he were a date who wasn't going to make it up to her place for a nightcap. Turning to him, she took a deep breath.

"Damon, I know none if this was your fault, but still I think I'd be more comfortable if I didn't see you for a while, okay?"

"Linda..."

She held her hand out. "I mean it, Damon. I've got to have some time."

"Fine."

She went inside. He watched the door close and then walked back to the bar.

He walked up to Broadway, stood at the intersection for a moment, glancing uptown and downtown like a man unsure of which way his destination was. When the light changed, he crossed Broadway and walked on down to Central Park. He entered the park and walked absently.

This wasn't a great section of the park. Gang kids gathered here and you didn't want to be here after dark and even the daylight wasn't as safe as it used to be. He didn't give a damn, though. Nobody was going to bother him. After all, he was the man with a gun, the man who'd spent four years going around Europe shooting people and who'd come home to shoot somebody else. Who gave a damn what time of day or night it was, give him a hard time and he'd blow your ass off with the .45 he had shoved in his belt right now.

He walked absently past the softball fields, turning right and heading in a vague downtown direction. He'd thought it as all behind him. He'd thought that when he got home that the shooting would stop, that he wouldn't see any more of those people with that look in their eyes, that expression that said they were already dead and wanted nothing more than to send a few people to hell before they arrived there.

He'd seen enough of those people and, damn it, he was afraid that he'd become one of them. When people looked at him, what did they see? What expression was carved into his face, what light shone through his eyes?

"Damn it, I didn't want to kill him. That was all behind me, you know, that was something I'd left back in Europe."

Lou Marsczyk scanned Taylor's face, shook his own head and said,

"Come in my office, all right?"

Taylor nodded and followed behind his editor. He noticed through the window that it had started raining, falling softly, little more than a fine mist. Come on, damn it, he thought, either rain or clear up, all right?

Great. Now he was angry at the weather.

"What's the problem, Taylor?" Marsczyk said.

"Funny, I thought I just told you the problem."

He took out the bottle of scotch, filled a couple of glasses and slid one across to Taylor. After tossing back a slug of his, he said, "So you had to kill a guy and you didn't like it."

"Christ, you make it sound like it as nothing, like I swatted a fly or something."

"That's about right. Take a good look at it and that's about what it is."

"It was a human life, Lou."

"Yeah, a human life that was all set to end yours. Let's get real, okay? You're saying you didn't want to kill him but if you hadn't, you think he'd be going through guilt feelings over killing you? Because that's the thing you want to keep in mind, old buddy, he was in that alley waiting to blow your ass off."

"I didn't say it made sense."

The rain was picking up. A breeze drove some drops through the open window. Both men ignored them. Taylor knew Marsczyk wasn't going to close the window. He hated not having air circulating around him. Let it build up to a hurricane and he might do something about it, but till then, the floor was going to get wet.

"Good thing you didn't. Look, I'd be disappointed in you if you weren't feeling something but, damn it, man, let's not go getting guilty about taking a guy like Mickey Arrelano off the streets."

"Knowing he was no good doesn't make me feel better. Maybe it should, but damn it, what the hell kind of thinking is that? The guy was no good, so we got the right to kill him?"

"You like your friend Linda, right?"

"Well, sure. What's that got to do with anything?"

"Just this. You think he was going to shoot you, let her watch him do it and then just let her walk away?"

Taylor felt heavy, as though the rain had entered his body, slogging him with weight. "I got to admit that never occurred to me."

"Think about it now." Marsczyk threw down the rest of his drink. "Tell you what: go out there and write up your notes. Give me everything you've got on this story, facts, ideas, opinions, everything. Let's see if we can figure out exactly what we're dealing with."

25

Sloppie Louie's, even though it was smaller than a Greenwich Village bedroom, was the most famous restaurant in the Fulton Fish Market. It sat no more than eighty people at long wooden tables and was mobbed from five in the morning till eight-thirty at night. When Taylor walked in, he glanced to his left where, next to the cigar store Indian, the cashier's desk stood.

Louie Morino looked up from behind the cash register and, with a big smile cracking the planes of his face, waved to Taylor, his trademark cloth napkin folded over his forearm.

"Damon," he called, as he crossed the room, "It's been too long, my friend."

"Way too long, Louie."

There were fingerprints all over the lenses of Louie's glasses. "Let me find you a seat."

"I'm meeting someone. Janie Hobson. You know her? She here yet?"

"A lovely girl. She's been coming in since she went to work at the market." He smiled once more. "So you're the guy she's waiting for. Lucky you, Damon."

When he was seated opposite her, Taylor said, "How's the job?"

She shrugged. "It isn't show business. I'm not quite sure yet whether that's good or bad."

They had to speak loudly. Louie's lunch crowd was huge, noisy, made up of characters from all over the city: market workers, Wall Street guys, people whose offices were in the neighborhood, shoppers in from the suburbs and a couple of the dozens of bums who depended on Louie for their meals.

Taylor watched Louie pass a sack of food to a small, crumpled man who wore a tattered topcoat despite the summer heat. "I love this place," he said.

"Me, too."

When the food came, both of them stopped talking, concentrating on the meal. All of the chatter around them came from people who had finished eating, Taylor noticed; when Louie placed a platter of fish in front of you, you gave it your full attention.

When they'd finished, Janie stirred sugar into her coffee and said, "Good as the company is, you didn't ask me here just to eat. What's on your mind?"

The job must be good for her, he thought. Her face seemed more relaxed and she'd done something he couldn't quite identify to her hair.

"A man tried to kill me the other night," he told her about the attack. "I got no idea who he was or why he was after me. I need help."

She shrugged helplessly. "I don't know how I can help."

"Brownie ever mention a man named Mickey Arrelano?"

"No," she said thoughtfully, "I don't think so. I don't recognize the name."

He took a picture from his inside pocket. "Recognize him?"

She shook his head. "I've never seen this man before." Studying the picture, she said, "He's dead, isn't he."

"It's the only picture I have."

"He's the one who tried to kill you?"

"Yes."

"And now he's dead."

Taylor hesitated. "Yes," he said flatly. Before she could say anything else, he continued, "Your husband ever mention a man named Mannie Francesca? He ever do any work for him?"

Her eyes narrowed. "I don't know that name. I don't think I've ever heard of him." She checked her watch. "I have to get back to work. I'm sorry I couldn't help you more."

"It's okay." He walked her to the door and then took the check over to Louie.

"Good looking hunk of womanhood." Louie said. "It's a pleasure to see her coming through the doors every day."

"Every day?"

"Sure. She works at Bragia's, next door. Where else is she going to eat lunch?"

"She doing okay there?"

Louie nodded like a waiter happy with his tip. "You worry because of what happened to her husband?"

"Don't you?"

"Of course. Relax. The boys take good care of her at Bragia's."

As Denise Hellman swept the apartment, Capote relaxed with his drink and tapped the cover of the copy of *Crime Scene* he was holding. "Might have been a touchy situation, but you got to admit it's a hell of a story."

It was an uncomfortable truth, Taylor thought, one of the things Damon Runyon hammered home to him: nothing counted but the story. It didn't matter if you faced death or lost everything you owned, if your wife and kids left you—always a region of your mind was saying *it's a hell of a story.*

How many times had he been around reporters who'd gone through hell for a story, been scared, injured, beaten and left for dead but had come back with that refrain—*it's a hell of a story.* Hell, during the war Ernie Pyle and the rest of them had gotten so deeply into the story that they'd wound up being killed by the enemy.

But they'd gotten one hell of a story.

He'd always thought he'd had better sense than that but it turned out he didn't. God help him, he was one of the breed, one of Damon Runyon's boys.

Denise Hellman came over and dropped four small plastic devices on the table. "You were right, Damon." Holding them up one at a time, she said, "This one was in your phone. This one came from your bedroom lamp. This one covered this room. They had it planted in your overhead light fixture and this one? In your bathroom."

"My, they are thorough, aren't they?" Capote said.

"That's everything?"

She wore blue jeans and a black tee shirt. Her hair was cut short, parted down the center, and she wore no makeup at all. "Until you leave the house again, yes. You're dealing with the feds, Damon. Assume that every time you go out, they come in."

"You're sure it's the feds?"

"This is sophisticated equipment. Local forces don't use it."

"How about the mobs?"

"Too subtle. They don't eavesdrop for information. They buy it."

"How do you know all this?" Capote asked.

"If Denise says it, you can take it to the bank," Taylor said. "Thanks, Denise. Usual fee?"

"For you, Damon? No increase."

After he wrote her a check, he turned to Capote. "Come on."

"Where we going?"

"The Stork Club."

"A night of revelry? Drunken debauchery. I didn't think that was your style, Damon."

Winchell loved Capote. He looked at him as though the little man were a toy created for his amusement.

"So, you're a writer, are you?"

Shyly—which surprised Taylor because he'd never seen Capote do anything shyly—Capote drew a manila envelope from his jacket pocket and handed it to Winchell, who accepted it as if it were a bribe.

"Here's a couple of my *New Yorker* stories."

"I can't wait to read them. I'll do it tonight, as soon as I put my column to bed."

Taylor was impressed. Handing Winchell your stories was a gutsy move, a refusal to play the fool the way everyone else in the city did for Winchell. Truman was signaling that he didn't intend to play by the house rules. He would not be one of the pack.

"I can tell you're a good writer," Winchell said. He signaled his waiter, who poured champagne for him and Capote and Irish whiskey for Taylor.

"Walter, I need a favor," Taylor said.

Winchell pushed his hat back. "If I can."

"My telephone's tapped and my apartment is bugged. I need for it to stop."

"There's some big stuff going down, Damon, and you're sitting right in the middle of it."

"And as long as I'm bugged and followed, I can't get out of the middle."

"You're upsetting a delicate balance."

"Can you call somebody about the bugs? And can you tell me who's behind it?"

Winchell called for another round. "Sure, but you don't need me to do anything like that. You're a good reporter and if you weren't one step away from the answer, you wouldn't have so many people pissed off. A day's legwork and you've got your answers." He paused. "The question is, what do you do when you get your answers?"

Taylor looked at him as if Winchell had suddenly begun speaking in tongues. "What do I do? I write the story, of course."

"And then?"

"Go on to the next one."

The Guy Lombardo Orchestra played something sweet and soothing, as dull and lifeless as a child's clay model. Dancers moved numbly across the floor, as if trying to stay awake. No one was going to confuse the Stork Club for Roseland.

"You know what's happening, don't you, Damon?"

"What's that?"

"You're becoming one of us. Runyon used to talk about it with me. He always said he hoped it wouldn't happen to you. He said you were too good to settle for being one of us."

Although Winchell hadn't noticed, Capote had his notebook out, propped in his lap and was writing in that crabbed, tiny and precise script of his. His eyes shifted from speaker to speaker as he followed the conversation, his face gleaming with pleasure.

"I'm a reporter, Walter," Taylor said. "Who wouldn't settle for that?"

"I don't think that's what Runyon meant, Damon."

26

Terri Louvin wouldn't answer her door. Taylor knocked again, waited and when nothing happened, called out, "Miss Louvin? It's Damon Taylor. Look, I know you're in there. I can hear the baby." Aware that her neighbors might be listening, he lowered his voice. "Let me in? I need to talk to you."

The first lock clicked open, followed by a second. The door slid open a few inches, still held by the chain, and Terri Louvin peeked out at him.

"Are you alone?" she said.

"Yeah. You all right?"

"Come in. Quick."

The blinds had not been opened so the apartment was dark. Toys were scattered among the dance equipment on the floor. A towel hung on the ballet bar and, even in the darkness, Taylor could see the mirror was streaked, dirty. It had been spotless when he'd been here before.

"What's going on?"

"I'm being evicted," she said.

"Christ, you're got to be months behind before they..." He read the pain in her eyes. "Brownie was making out the rent checks?"

"No, Brownie was not making out the rent checks, Damon. That's the problem. Brownie left me two weeks before he got shot. At least I assume he left me. He went out and didn't come back. The thing is, he hadn't paid a bill for months when he left. He claimed to be on top of the bills but he wasn't paying anybody." She indicated the apartment with a wave. "You can see I don't have a phone anymore."

"You're working, aren't you?"

"I'm pulling in thirty-five bucks a week," she said flatly. "I pay twenty in child care and I owe six hundred in rent. At the rate I'm paying it down, I should be even by about 1964." She took a deep breath. "I don't want to sound cynical or defeated or anything, but I don't know what to do." Glancing toward the bedroom, she said, "I can't be out on the streets. I've got a baby."

"How 'bout I lend you some money?"

She was a small girl, barely over five feet tall, with a dancer's body—lithe, well-muscled, and lean. Her calves were as well developed a body-builder's.

"Don't you do that. Don't go offering me money."

"Why not? You need it, I've got it."

"Why not? Because I'm just about desperate enough to take it and I don't need the complications."

"No complications, Terri. I don't want a damn thing out of you. You'd be amazed what they pay me on that damn magazine. I'm telling you, it's a fortune. Let me use a little of the excess to help you out."

"It's not right. I don't even know you."

"Don't worry about it."

"I won't sleep with you. All you're going to get is your money back."

"That's all I want."

As he wrote out a check for fifteen hundred dollars and placed it in her palm, he supposed he ought to feel really good about doing this, but really he didn't feel anything out of the ordinary. She folded the check and slid it into her pocket without looking at the amount.

"Let me get to why I'm here," he said.

"You didn't just stop by to bail me out."

"These photos are a little gruesome but I need to know if you know this guy."

She recoiled as she glanced at the picture. "That is... was, rather, Mickey Arrelano. I saw him around with Brownie a few times."

"He and Brownie work together?"

"I don't know. They hit the streets together, I know that. Brownie said he'd known him for years." She shook her head. "I'm sorry I can't help you more."

"You helped a lot. Look, you need any more money, you let me know, okay?"

"This'll do. Believe me, this will do." Her smile came more easily this time. "I swear, I'll pay you back."

When the doorbell rang, Taylor opened it to see the hunchback of Notre Dame.

"Sanctuary, sanctuary," Quasimodo said in a broken voice.

O'Bradovich wasn't really Quasimodo; he was Charles Laughton as Quasimodo. His face was disfigured, his right eye huge and bulging, and the hump on his back caused him to look as gnarled and bent as a dying oak tree.

"Hell, man, I'd give you sanctuary any day."

O'Bradovich tried to smile but the makeup froze his face. He could only manage a stark grimace. "Sanctuary, hell. Just pour me a drink, man."

"Come on in." When he got inside, he ripped off his shirt. The hump came off with it and he stood straighter. "That's better. Jesus, how did Laughton spend eight weeks in a rig like that?" He let the harness fall. It thumped when it hit the floor.

"Uncomfortable?"

"Let's just say you don't have to act the posture."

Taylor poured a couple of drinks. "You're still wearing the eye."

"You know how long I worked on that thing?"

The whiskey was as welcome as lemonade on a July afternoon. "How'd you know how to do a thing like that?"

"I didn't. Thing is, if you're out to learn this art, you take a model, like Laughton as Quasimodo, and instead of asking how they did it, you ask how can I do it. Nine times out of ten, you find out how they did it."

Taylor wondered how long it was going to take for O'Bradovich to wake up and start doing the work he really loved. Sure, the man went up for acting jobs, but his real passion was creating makeup effects. The producers of *Tom Corbett, Space Cadet* had offered him a job not long ago, doing makeup on the show, creating aliens, and O'Bradovich carried on as if the offer was an insult, beneath his dignity.

"All it's got going for it is money," he said. "It's a ton of money, sure, but I'm an artist, you know? Me on an afternoon kiddie show? I don't think so."

"If they offered you an acting job, would you take that?"

"Oh, hell, yes. In a minute."

The huge eye, red-rimmed and bloodshot, did not move. Though it was obvious how fake the eye was, after you'd looked at it for a few minutes, it took on a sense of reality. It stared at you.

"I didn't get the Miller play," O'Bradovich said. "They went with Kennedy."

"Too bad."

The phone rang. When he answered it, Winchell spoke as loudly and quickly as he did on the radio. "Brogan and Brigati were bugging you. They were acting on their own initiative, with no permission, no warrant, nothing. They won't be bothering you again."

"You're sure of that?"

"They've been transferred. Somewhere in Oregon, I understand."

"Thanks, Walter."

"That's all right, but, Damon?"

"Yeah?"

"You're still in trouble."

"I know. Walter, I appreciate what you've done and I wouldn't think of asking you for anything else."

"You know I'd do anything for you, Damon."

Winchell could make the promises now that he knew he wouldn't have to deliver on them. Give the man his way of viewing himself, his dignity; he didn't have anything else.

"I know, Walter, thanks."

Taylor uncoiled the cord and put the phone down. O'Bradovich looked curious but didn't say anything. When Taylor didn't volunteer any information, O'Bradovich poured himself another drink.

"I tell you NBC offered me a job?"

"What's the part?"

"It's not acting. They want me to be makeup coordinator on all their live shows, you know, *Philco Playhouse*, the rest of them. They're doing more and more live plays and what they told me is they need a man of vision to oversee the makeup effects."

"Beats the hell out of *Tom Corbett*, doesn't it?"

"Eternity in hell beats *Tom Corbett*. Still, I'm an actor, you know? I only developed the makeup skills to help my acting career."

"Sometimes we don't know what's best for us. We let what we want get in the way of what we need."

"You sound like a bar full of French Existentialists."

"It's true, though. Capote wrote a story about it."

Taylor could see that the discomfort he was feeling came from O'Bradovich's neediness. The man reeked of a need for someone else to make this decision for him. When the phone rang again, Taylor grabbed it.

"Mr. Taylor," the voice on the line said, "this is Leo Salmon."

"How are you, Mr. Salmon?"

"An associate of mine wants to meet with you. If I send a car, can you be available in half an hour?"

"Is it important?"

"I understand there was an attempt on your life? My associate wants to discuss that. He may have information you need. Does that make it important?" He hesitated and then added, "I promise safe passage both ways."

"You need my address?"

"I know where you live."

I'll bet you do, Taylor thought.

27

Pete Brescher trotted over and flopped down next to Taylor on the stoop. The kid was small for his age, with freckles and shaggy light hair that always needed trimming. He held a Dodgers cap in his hand. Noticing Taylor scan the traffic, the kid kept his eyes focused on the turn off of Broadway.

"How you doing, Mr. Taylor?"

"Pretty good, Pete. Been out to the stadium lately? Seen any games?"

"Nope. How 'bout you?"

"Been too busy. Tell you what: when the workload lightens, we'll go see the Dodgers."

"Great!"

The same black Cadillac that had taken him to Salmon's Brooklyn house made the turn and glided down the street. The kids gathering for the evening stickball game jumped out of the way at the last possible moment, while Taylor stood. The car came to a stop in front of his building. Joseph Levinson stepped out and opened the back door.

"Mr. Taylor?"

"See you later, Pete."

"Jesus," the kid ran down the stoop with him. "That's the new Cadillac, ain't it?"

"Yeah,"

"How the hell'd he get that? They ain't on the market yet. You got to wait till winter for one." Pete dashed to the curb to check the car out.

"See you, Pete," Taylor said as he climbed inside.

Levinson undid the emergency brake and drove off. "That your son?"

"Just a friend. Lives in the building."

"You don't ever hear an adult call a kid a friend."

Taylor said, "Wouldn't know another way to describe him."

"So you don't have any kids? I'm about to have my first. My wife's eight months pregnant."

"You must be really happy."

"Yeah, when I'm not scared to death."

"It's fine. What's to be scared of?"

"Mr. Taylor, I lost my bowling ball the other night. If I can't keep up with a bowling ball..."

"Relax. Your wife will teach you everything you need to know." He saw they weren't headed to Brooklyn. "Where are you taking me anyway?"

"Just over to the East Side. We're almost there."

He drove a couple of blocks downtown, made a left and pulled over to the curb in front of a townhouse. As he waited for Levinson to open his door, Taylor noticed that the windows, even those on the upper floors, were barred. The house looked like an expensive private reform school.

"I'll be waiting for you here," Levinson said.

"I can get back easily enough. Go on home to your wife."

Levinson brightened. "You don't mind?"

"Go."

"Thanks."

The Cadillac was turning the corner by the time Taylor rang the bell. He heard the sound of locks being opened and, after a moment, the door opened. A man in butler's livery scanned Taylor carefully. Taylor was pretty sure buttling wasn't the man's main occupation.

"You Taylor?"

"Yeah."

"Come on in." The man frisked him as he walked by. "I'll take you to the boss."

The boss was in the living room, listening to George Burns and Gracie Allen on the console radio, a fresh drink resting on the table next to his chair. Even relaxing at home, he wore an impeccably cut suit and a tie that complemented it. That stood to reason; Frank Costello was known for his attention to his wardrobe. Not long ago, Taylor had been covering him at a trial. Costello's lawyer was giving him a hard time because Costello insisted on wearing a $350 suit to court. He was making a bad impression on the jury, the lawyer said, he had to dress down.

"You got to wear clothes off the rack."

Costello snorted. "I'd rather blow the Goddamn case."

Now he stood slowly, walked over and shook Taylor's hand.

"Glad you could come." He searched Taylor's face as if looking for a weakness. "Jameson's, isn't it?"

"That'll do."

As he took the seat Costello indicated, Taylor reviewed what he knew about the man. He'd been born in Italy as Francesco Castiflia, but the family name had become Costello as soon as they came to the states and settled in East Harlem. When he was fourteen, Frank robbed his landlady, who recognized him, called the cops and set in motion the pattern that guided his criminal career right then and there by beating the rap. It wasn't till he was twenty-four that he was actually convicted of something—carrying a gun—and sent to prison for a year. Now, though he'd done enough big time crime to accumulate thousands of years behind bars, he'd never served another day. The papers called him the man who could not be convicted.

If he couldn't, it was because he and his partners Meyer Lansky and Lucky Luciano had begun buying cops back during prohibition. Now, Costello owned whole police departments but that was nothing when you considered that he had learned early on that J. Edgar Hoover lived and died by how the ponies ran. Costello fed him a steady stream of winners and Hoover decided that organized crime was a myth.

As he thought of all this, Taylor wondered why he'd been called here. Had he somehow become important enough to be a thorn in Costello's side? If so, he wasn't very happy about it; Costello made more people disappear than Houdini.

"You know who I am?"

Costello was a big man with bags under beady eyes and a flattened nose. The expensive suits didn't do a thing to make him look handsome.

"Everybody knows who you are, Frank."

Costello took a deep breath and stared at Taylor longer than was necessary. "Why do you call me by my first name? We don't know each other. We ain't friends. Why do you not show me respect?"

"Sorry, Mr. Costello."

Costello nodded, a king acknowledging a commoner. "You're getting to be a problem for some friends of mine, Taylor."

"Is that a fact, Costello?"

Anger flushed Costello's face but he pulled it under control and said, "I see your point, Mr. Taylor."

"Mr. Costello, I don't want to make things tough for your friends. If that's happening, it's not my intention."

"I can't be bothered with intentions." He watched his butler put a tray of drinks on the table. "What is it you want, anyway?"

"The truth."

"What do you mean?"

"Somebody fed me Arrelano like a plate of spaghetti. Even if he shot Brownie—which I don't believe for a minute—there were two shooters. They only fed me one."

"So the truth about that shooting is that important to you? Even if I tell you it's got nothing to do with any of my activities?"

"It's got something to do with you or we wouldn't be sitting here. Look, Mr. Costello, these days the truth is all we got. The war took everything else."

"I don't follow."

"Without the truth, nothing means anything. It's all a game."

"You know what the truth is?"

"What's that?"

"It's some stupid shit Tommy Lucchese believes. He says the dumbest fucking stuff you can imagine and then swears it's the truth."

"To me, it's all I got."

"How much?"

"What?"

Costello swirled his drink. "What's it going to take to get you out of this?"

They'd been in the room for ten minutes and he'd felt the danger level rise with each passing second. The safe passage guaranteed him his trip home, but what about tomorrow? How long did it extend?

"I told you my price."

"The truth. What are you, some modern day Diogenes?"

Taylor raised his eyebrows.

"Of course, Mr. Taylor, I know who Diogenes is." He looked over at the radio as though he were getting bored. "Here's what else I know. I brought you here in good faith and gave you every chance to save your life."

"All I've got on my side is *Crime Scene*. Anything happens to me and a hundred reporters are going to be crawling over you like ants. You got a secret, they'll find it. You got stuff you don't want anybody to know, they'll report it."

"I know the risk. Still, it's up to you now. If you don't find a way to get yourself out of this, it's not going to go well for you." He saluted him with his drink. "You're a strong man, Mr. Taylor. Any other circumstances, I'd admire you for that."

28

When he got home, Taylor found a note slipped under his door:

> Damon,
> Wanted to talk to you but you're out tonight. I'm taking the NBC job.
> Sometimes it takes a long time for a man to see what he was born to do instead of what he wants to do.
> You can buy me a celebration drink tomorrow.
>
> Bob

Something about the phrase O'Bradovich had used, about doing what you were born to do, resonated, but he couldn't make it fall into place. He was too far gone. Right now, all he could handle was a nightcap and a good night's sleep

When he woke the next morning, he knew Winchell had been right: the answers had been right there in front of him. Now he had the rest of the story. He knew exactly what had happened to Brownie Hobson and why.

He still had a couple of problems. For one thing, he didn't really have any proof. Most important, though, he didn't have any idea what he was going to do about it. If he didn't play this one right, he could bring Costello down on him.

He took the elevator up to the fourth floor of the Brill Building and hurried down the hall till he found Ronnie Hamilton's door. When he flung it open, Hamilton looked up from his desk, saw Taylor and pulled back, his sudden movement causing the chair to hit the wall.

"Jesus, Taylor, what do you want?"

"You're a lot nervous, Ronnie."

"Damn right, I'm nervous. You come around, people get dead."

"Relax, Hamilton. All I need out of you is a picture."

Hamilton's office—a rabbit hutch—showed he wasn't doing well. When the music business types who worked out of the building hit it big, they took suites on the upper floors. When they rolled the dice on the wrong singer or the wrong song, they moved downstairs to offices like this one.

"A picture?"

"I want a glossy of your first PR shots for the Lindy Hoppers. The original cast."

He scratched his head like Stan Laurel. "Damon, I don't have those anymore."

Taylor's voice was calm. "It would be in your best interests to come up with one."

"Let me check the file cabinet."

In the first drawer he opened, Hamilton came up with a file folder that held a dozen eight by tens. He passed it over to Taylor.

"I only need one."

"Hell, take 'em all," Hamilton said, "What the hell am I going to do with them?"

Big Joe Turner held the mic close to his mouth with his right hand. He stood on the bandstand, a glass of beer in his left hand and sang softly, gently, as if he didn't want to blow his voice out in this rehearsal. A piano player accompanied him.

When he saw Taylor come in, Big Joe shouted, "Hey, my man. Vann, take five, my man's here."

He wrapped Taylor in a bear hug. "Ain't seen you around, man."

"Figured you'd seen enough of me by now."

"Never," Turner laughed. "Hey, that piece you wrote on me? My phone ain't stopped ringing. You made me sound like a blend of Jimmy Witherspoon and God." He turned to the piano player "Hey, Vann, meet Damon Taylor. Damon, that's Vann Walls. He's the piano man."

Walls played an arpeggio to acknowledge the nickname and continued to play as Taylor and Turner walked over to the bar. Settling in with a couple of drafts, Taylor said, "Need a quick favor, Joe."

"Name it."

"Remember telling me about Brownie Hobson hitting a girl?"

Turner shook his head. "I ain't likely to forget that, man. You don't treat a lady like that. Not for no reason."

Taylor laid an eight by ten on the bar. "Is the woman in this picture?"

Turner finished off his beer and tapped one of the women on the chest. "Hell, here she is, right here."

"You sure?"

"Hell, yes, I'm sure. Why? This important?"

"You might say so. You just solved a murder."

Energy built in him until Taylor felt like a radio whose battery had just been changed. Now, he thought, all he had to do was find a way to use what he had and keep himself alive.

It was a hot evening and Mannie Francesca's shirt had sweated through beneath his suit coat. He wanted to take his jacket off but then everybody'd see the gun in his waistband. So he followed along, half a block behind Taylor, using the light crowd as cover. When Taylor stopped in a bar, Mannie hung out across the street and waited, sweltering in the heat—which he didn't mind because by God Taylor was going to pay for it. A tiny man in a white suit left the bar with Taylor, chattering away as they walked uptown. That complicated things a little but not much. He'd just pop them both.

Costello would be pissed. This afternoon he had pulled Francesca in for lunch and had given him a hard time. Rolling his fat head, Costello adjusted his pinkie ring and said, "Mannie, Mannie," like he was disappointed, "how'd you let it get this bad?"

"It just didn't work out like I planned."

"That's because you planned bad and now, because of your asshole planning, we can't do a damn thing. He knows too much now and if anything happens to him, all his fucking reporters are going to jump on the story."

Mannie tried to look properly contrite but he was wondering if Costello had any idea that any day now, Francesca was going to pop him and take over. The only reason the fat bastard was still alive was because Francesca needed to learn the business. Soon as he'd picked up a few more intricacies, Costello was a squirrel on the side of the road.

"I'll take care of it, Mr. Costello."

"Don't hit him. Not till the papers lose interest in him."

"I'll buy him off."

"You got to be subtle about it. Things are different now, you know."

These old guys, to them, it was the same world it had been at the turn of the century, when they'd dragged their fucking donkeys and pushcarts off the boats. Now they looked up and saw the electric light and said, "It's all different now."

"I'll take care of it."

"Mannie, you don't want to lose your head over this. Don't let it get personal."

"It's okay."

"Remember, she's a very pretty lady who won't like having to go on without you if you fuck this thing up."

Now, as he followed Taylor and the little guy, he realized that Costello had been threatening him. His own life was on the line now. All right. He'd take these guys out and then go back and pop Costello, show him who was the one to be issuing threats. So he followed Taylor and the little guy down into the subway, picturing Costello's fat face quivering as he begged for his life. While Francesca put a bullet through that double chin of his and got blood all over that expensive suit.

The subway platform was hot enough to make the streets above seem like paradise and the reek of stale sweat overwhelmed the place. He hadn't been down in one of these since he'd stopped working the streets. He breathed as shallowly as he could as he walked slowly toward the opposite end where Taylor was now leaning forward, checking the tunnel to see if the train was coming. The little guy rocked on his heels, his hands in his pockets.

Capote continued to rock on his heels, as if that would make the train come faster. His hands were jammed into the pockets of his trench coat. Standing to Taylor's right, he said, "You know, staring down the track won't make the train get here any sooner."

"That a fact?"

"For sure."

He watched the only other man on the platform, a greasy looking guy, stroll toward them.

Across the tracks, a couple of guys passed a bottle back and forth as they waited for the downtown train. Francesca dismissed them; no problem there. Reaching into his pocket, he closed his hand around his Police Special. He strolled over and, just before Taylor appeared to sense his presence behind him, eased the pistol out. It had almost cleared the pocket when the little guy shouted, "Look out!"

Everything went crazy. Taylor dropped to the floor and rolled while the little guy somehow had a tiny silver automatic in his hand and was pumping off shots at Francesca as fast as he could pull the trigger. The shots popped like firecrackers. Francesca jumped back as bullets whizzed around him, one slicing the cloth of his suit coat, and by the time he'd recovered, he was staring into the barrel of Taylor's .45 and as his mouth dropped open, felt a shock huge enough to numb him. From a place deep in his unconscious, a recess of his mind he'd never visited, he was aware that he was sailing through the air, landing on his back and, as he tried to speak, to cry out in pain, he heard the shots for the first time. The sound of the shots was the last thing he heard.

"Taylor, ain't you getting tired of shooting hoods?" McCall said.

They'd cleared the subway platform, hauled the body away, and gotten statements from the drunks across the tracks. Taylor and Capote had gone downtown to give McCall their statements. When it was all done at two in the morning, the three of them walked up to Irish Jack's which, since it was a cop's bar, didn't have to worry about closing time.

"Fact is," Taylor said, "If Truman here hadn't been on his toes, I'd be the dead man instead of Francesca."

McCall turned to Capote. "What the hell you doing carrying that popgun, anyway?"

Capote sipped his drink through a straw. "Oh, I always carry it."

"You never told me you carried a gun," Taylor said.

"It never came up." He signaled for another drink. "After a while you don't even notice it's there. A friend of mine in New Orleans gave it to me, said if I was going to New York, I was going to need it." Flashing McCall a big smile, he said, "Looks like she was right. Of course, I can't hit the Flatiron Building from the sidewalk, but it shook him up, didn't it?"

The night had gotten as long as a Thomas Wolfe novel. Taylor was falling apart with tiredness. "What amazes me," Taylor said, "was how bad Francesca was. He was so obvious following us, he might as well have been wearing a clown suit."

"He underestimated you, all right," McCall said.

"If he'd been a radio," Capote said, "you wouldn't even be a station on his dial. He didn't give you any credit at all."

When the knock came at the door, Taylor glanced out the window before answering it. Leo Salmon's Cadillac sat double-parked, taking up the westbound lane. Levinson, in full uniform, stood between the car and Pete Brescher's stickball team, who were enthralled by the car. Taylor could hear their excited chatter.

He opened the door. Leo Salmon and Janie Hobson stood in the doorway. "Come on in," Taylor said.

He'd spent the morning working the phones, waiting for callbacks and when they'd come in, made the final call of the morning to Leo Salmon.

"I was just about to call you," Salmon said.

"Oh?"

"Relax. Francesca had specific orders to leave you alone. He went out on his own. You don't have to worry about any repercussions."

"This is from the top?"

"From the top. You're okay."

"He made a try for me after Frank told him not to? How'd he expect to survive that?"

"The only way he could would be by taking out Frank, too. He must have been making his move. The fool thought it was still the twenties, when you shot your way to the top. In a weird way, you did Frank a favor."

"I'm about to try and do him another one. Can you have a meeting?"

"Sounds provocative. Sure."

"And, Leo?"

"Yeah?"

"Can you bring Janie Hobson along?"

Janie Hobson appeared unhappy to be here. She huddled by the picture of Taylor with Damon Runyon and Duke Snider. Salmon sized the apartment up, looking wistful, as if his memories of living in a place like this weren't all bad.

"Something to drink?" Taylor said.

"A shot of that Jameson's you're so fond of wouldn't hurt," Salmon said. "Janie? Something for you?"

"Leo...."

"It won't take long, Janie. Drink?"

She nodded, her face tight, closed off. Her mouth was tight, as if she'd decided that since speaking hadn't worked, she'd commit to silence.

Taylor passed out the drinks. Salmon checked out the room, his eyes stopping on Taylor's radio-record player.

"That's some unit you got there. What is it, a Dupont?"

"It's a good one. Record player's got great sound with the lowest turntable rumble I could find."

"You use diamond needles?"

"Of course."

Salmon nodded. "Radio reception?"

"On a clear night I can pull in Philadelphia."

"That's great. Where I am, I can hardly bring in Manhattan stations. Too much building bounce."

"Got an antenna on the roof?"

"That what you do?"

Janie slammed her drink glass down. "Can we get on with it?"

"Relax, Janie." He turned to Taylor, "By the way, I've got fifteen percent of *Finian's Rainbow*."

"Leo, please..."

"Janie's right. Let's get to it. What did you want to see us about, Damon?"

"I know what happened to Brownie Hobson."

"So do I. He got himself shot."

"I know who and why."

"Why tell me?" Now that the pleasantries are out of the way, Salmon's held himself differently. His posture was more aggressive, as if he were ready to strike like a snake.

"We'll get to why in a minute. First I have to tell you a story." He polished off his drink. "I was looking at the whole thing through the wrong lens. Like everybody else, I assumed the fashion house was central. The cops were thinking that way, so I bought into it."

"They weren't connected?"

"If there was a connection, it was secondary at best. That would have been Mannie's thing."

"Mannie Francesca?"

"You said one of your associates was having an affair with Janie. That was Francesca, wasn't it?"

"Leo, you didn't..." Janie's voice was small.

He signaled her for silence. To Taylor, he said, "You're telling the story."

"Janie, I can produce a ton of people who saw you with Mannie but you told me you didn't know him. Later on, in passing, you mentioned you'd met him."

"All right. I knew him. That doesn't mean I killed him."

"Yeah," Salmon interrupted, "what's the big deal?"

"The deal is she lied, which means she had reason to lie," Taylor said. "It means I know who the shooters were."

Salmon clasped his hands in front of him. "You might want to stop right here."

"Damon?" Janie looked at him as if he were a cockroach. "You saying I killed him?"

"You and Francesca."

Salmon stepped between them. "You know where this is likely to end up, don't you, Damon? We can still back off but if you go any further..."

"Hear it all before you say anything, all right, Leo?" Taylor said. "Funny, one of my neighbors left a note on my door about seeing things the way they were, instead of the way you wanted them to be. That made me look at the case differently and everything fell together. When I figured it was Janie, I turned my research department loose and you'd be amazed what a first-rate research department like we've got down at the magazine can come up with. They've been calling me with verification all day. Francesca wants Brownie out of the way, probably because of the Very Kelly thing and the way he's been treating Janie, too. He's holding off because Janie doesn't want her ex-husband hit. Even if he's the prime bastard of the universe, she doesn't want him dead till he beat her up. That changed everything. Am I right, Janie?"

"Leo, can we leave now?"

"It's always personal, Leo, you know that. That's what I forgot. It's always personal. It isn't who profits by the killing, it's who wanted the bastard dead."

"Damon," Salmon suggested, "are you suggesting she had Mannie hit him?"

"Come on, Leo, she did it herself. She's the first shooter, Francesca's the second. I figure she tells Mannie she wants to kill Brownie and he says, "Let's do it." She's got one reason for wanting him dead, Mannie's got a dozen: he did it out of love, because of the Vera Kelly thing, and, knowing Mannie, probably because he figured it would be good to have something big to hold over Janie if she ever decides to leave him. With Mannie, who the hell knows?"

Janie said, "You can't prove any of this."

"So far. But if I turn all the resources of my magazine lose on you, Janie, how long do you think you'll last?" To Salmon, he said, "Horace McCall's a good cop with a lot of clout. Turn him loose on this, the whole house is going to tumble."

"Damon, Damon," Salmon sounded disappointed, "you're not a stupid man. You have to know you're putting your life on the line. Costello sees everything he's been building start to crumble like a cookie, what do you think he's going to do to you?"

"I'd be a fool if it didn't trouble me."

"You're in way over your head. While you were doing all this research, didn't you ever ask yourself why Frank gives a damn about a second rate dancer's wife?"

"Because she's family. She's his niece. And we all know how important family is to Frank."

"You think he's going to let you blow the whistle on his flesh and blood?"

"You said I'm in over my head. You're right. And I want out. I don't want to blow the whistle on Janie."

"You don't?"

"Janie, I know why you did what you did. Christ, I might have done it myself. Way he treated you, it's a wonder he lived as long as he did. The man abandoned you, he abandoned Terri Louvin, I don't want to see you burn."

"He left Terri? And the baby?"

"Hadn't been home in two weeks."

"Agreed, Taylor, he was a son of a bitch. What do you want?" Salmon said.

"A deal."

"A deal." Salmon sounded a little sad, as though he were disappointed in Taylor. "I suppose you've protected yourself? The letter with the lawyer, the witness statements, the rest of it?"

"All the way down the line."

"What do you have in mind?" Salmon poured himself another drink. "How much do you want?"

"Let's talk about what I don't want first. I can't stop you guys from taking over the Garment District, I can't stop Costello from sewing up cops and politicians. That's going to happen. Sooner or later, he'll go too far and the feds will have to take him down. When it does, I'll write about it. But I'm not about to try to stop him myself."

"Like I said," Salmon said, "what do you want?"

"There's a girl. Terri Louvin..."

Janie said, "the one he left me for?"

"She's a good kid, Janie. It's not her fault."

Leo Salmon furrowed his brow. "You mean the girlfriend? The one with the baby?"

"Leo, Terri Louvin got burned bad by this whole thing. She's out there with a baby and doesn't have a dollar to her name. She's about to be thrown out of her apartment. Janie, you're covered. Frank's going to take care of you, but this girl's got an eight month old baby, no money, no job, no nothing. Brownie treated her the way he treated you, used her up like a tissue and tossed her in the corner."

"It's a tough town," Salmon said, "happens to a lot of girls."

"Stop it, Leo," Janie said. "She's a good kid. Jesus, she's just as young and stupid as I was when I met Brownie. She's not the only girl stupid enough to buy the crap Brownie was handing out."

"Bottom line, Taylor. What do you want?"

"She's a classically trained dancer. It'd be nice if she had a dance school."

"Say that again?"

"I want her to have a dance school. Hers, not yours, and I want it to succeed. I want this girl to have a future."

"And you? What do you want for yourself?"

"I'm okay. I don't need a thing."

"Nothing?"

"Like I said, I'm doing okay."

"What's this girl to you?"

"Nothing. The way I see it, she and Janie are the real victims here. Janie's covered. I want this girl covered, too."

Salmon frowned. "You're a strange man, Damon. Let me see if I got this right: the Louvin girl gets a dance school, all this goes away?"

"Take care of her and here's the story I write: Mickey Arrelano's the first shooter, Mannie's the second. They did the guys at Vera Kelly's, too. We'll go with the cops' theory: Brownie saw the shooting at Vera Kelly's, so they popped him, too. Why all the shooting over there? Who knows? Maybe a homosexual triangle or something. All the principals are dead, we'll never know. What we do know is it's cleared."

"That's the story you'll write?"

"Yeah."

"Frank told me you wouldn't settle for less than the truth. What happened to that?"

Taylor put down his drink. "Frank also said every man's got his price. I guess we found mine."

"Funny how your price doesn't put a penny in your pocket."

Taylor shrugged.

"I wouldn't think a man that learned his trade from Damon Runyon would do a deal like this."

"I don't know, maybe it's exactly what he'd do."

Salmon turned to Janie Hobson. "It affects you, too, Janie. You have to approve it."

"You know what I'm thinking?"

"What's that?"

"I got lousy taste in men. Uncle Frank told me he ordered Mannie to leave Taylor here alone. He went after him anyway. You know how Uncle Frank gets when a direct order is disobeyed. There's only one way Mannie could have hoped to get away with this."

"He intended to hit Costello, too?" Taylor said. He wanted to be taking notes.

"That's right. Anything I felt for him died when he decided he was bigger than my family. And Terri? She's a good kid. If we can give her a break, why not?"

Salmon put down his glass. "It's too big for me to sign off on. I'll have to take it to Frank."

As the sound of the crowd died down and the announcer finished raving about Jackie Robinson's home run, the phone rang. When Taylor picked it up, Joseph Levinson greeted him.

"How's your wife?" Taylor said.

"Big as a Macy's parade float. Mr. Salmon asked me to call. He said you're got a deal. Draw up a letter spelling the details out, just as you told them to Mr. Salmon. Give me a call when it's ready. I'll pick it up."

A letter put him on record, gave Costello access to him. Nothing he could do about that. You went to these guys for a deal, you had to expect it to cost something.

"Thank him for me."

"I will. By the way, you know that Brescher kid, lives in your building?"

"He's a good kid. Why?"

"Tell him Mr. Salmon wants his hubcaps back."

29

Terri Louvin called him at the office a few days later. "Damon, the most wonderful thing has happened." Her voice was alive and vibrant.

"Is that right? What is it?"

"I've got a job."

"A job?"

Marsczyk stuck his head out the door, saw Taylor and waved him into the office. Taylor gave him a five minute signal.

"Not just a job, Damon, a wonderful job. I'm going to be managing a new dance school. I'm the boss. I run the place. The pay's good, too. I'll have enough to hire a nanny to go to work with me. I'll even be able to pay you back."

"Want to tell me about the job over lunch?"

"I don't have a baby sitter."

"Bring him along. We'll go to the automat in your neighborhood. Babies aren't a problem there."

"Sounds fine."

"One o'clock?"

"Too close to nap time. Make it noon?"

He was dialing Leo Salmon's number when Marsczyk leaned out again. "Where's your copy?"

"It's coming." When he got Salmon on the line, he said, "Terri Louvin just told me she got a job managing a dance school. That's not what we agreed to."

"Damon, Damon," Salmon said wearily, "use your head. We can't just call the girl up and give her a school. Look, in six months or so, the owners are going to want to sell out, move to Miami Beach or something. The Louvin girl's going to buy them out. She'll get the school, the building, the whole thing."

"She'll never be able to afford that."

"Maybe Brownie Hobson's will's going to turn up, leave her a bunch of money nobody knew he had. Trust me, it's going to be fine."

"Sounds good, Mr. Salmon."

"Leo to my friends, Damon."

He hadn't thought of himself as Leo Salmon's friend. It fit, though. You can't make a deal with the devil without becoming a devil yourself.

"See you around, Leo."

When he handed in his copy, he told Marsczyk he was quitting. Marsczyk sat behind his desk, his lips pursed, head nodding and, without taking his eyes off the pages he was reading, poured each of them a drink.

"To the future," he said.

"Thanks."

"What are you going to do?"

"I don't know. Go back to a daily, write a book, climb a mountain, who knows? Maybe I won't do anything for a while.

"It's been good, Damon."

"It has."

"Why you leaving?"

"It's time, that's all."

"Not entirely clear, Damon."

"Best I can do."

"How 'bout we think of it as a leave of absence? Open-ended."

"I don't think I'll be back."

"We'll see. Good luck"

As he walked out of the office, it crossed his mind that Marsczyk hadn't been all that surprised by his resignation. He acted as though he'd expected it. The office door opened behind him and Marsczyk leaned out, waving Taylor's copy.

"Damon?" he called.

"Yeah?"

He held out the copy and said, "You ever going to tell me what really went down? Maybe over a drink sometime?"

"Maybe," he said.

Without looking back, he walked out of the office. The weather had broken. The day was sunny and cool and the breeze felt good on his face as he headed uptown.

The End

AFTERWORD

Although *Damon Runyon's Boys* is a work of fiction, it does have a foundation in fact and, although the facts shouldn't interfere with reading pleasure, much of the background of the novel is true. The bars, restaurants and other places used for local color existed. Cops and reporters really hung out in the places they frequent in the novel.

The three major crime families did fight throughout for control of the garment district. Frank Costello won the fight and his Luciano crime family ran the district until the seventies when a federal crime force finally managed to clean up the district.

The biographical details about Costello are accurate. After the events in the novel, Costello's luck took a bad turn. In 1951, a Senate Committee investigating organized crime grilled him on live TV for eight days. Costello made one of his few strategic errors. As a condition of testimony, he insisted his face not be seen on TV.

The networks, recognizing good TV when they saw it, focused the cameras on his hands. Viewers watched the gangster rasp answers while twisting his hands nervously. The PR effects were devastating. On March 15, 1951, Costello, recognizing he'd lost the public relations war, claimed he had a sore throat and refused to continue testifying. He was convicted of contempt of Congress and sentenced to eighteen months.

While he was away, Vito Genovese took over by the simple expedient of hitting everyone who had been loyal to Costello. When Costello suggested he come back to work, Genovese ordered a hit on him. It was botched, but Costello got the message and retired. He lived quietly on Long Island until his death at the age of 82 in 1957.

Truman Capote was a reporter for *PM* in the late forties. By his own admission, he was one of the worst reporters in the history of American journalism. He left the newspaper business and became Truman Capote, writer, celebrity, and friend to the women of high society.

Walter Winchell remained the king of pseudo-journalism until he tried to take his act to television. One of the keys to his radio success was the staccato presence of a rapid fire teletype machine which accompanied his equally rapid fire voice. The fantasy was a man ripping off the wire items and feeding them straight through to us: news as it was happening. What viewers saw, though, was a tired old man, clicking away on a teletype key while he spat out items. The impression was ludicrous enough to drive away the few people who still took him seriously. He finished his career as the narrator of *The Untouchables*, a hyper-violent TV show that starred a wooden Robert Stack as a romanticized version of Elliot Ness, the man who finally brought down Al Capone.

Bob O'Bradovich had a long and distinguished career creating makeup effects for NBC and in the early fifties, Big Joe Turner was amazed and amused to find himself one of the founding fathers of rock and roll when he recorded such classics as *Shake, Rattle and Roll*, *Chains of Love* and *Honey Hush*. As he enjoyed his late career success, he frequently commented on how strange it was to discover that all of those years, he'd been a rock and roll singer—even before rock existed.

□ □ □

In the film *The Man Who Shot Liberty Valance*, a newspaper editor discovers the truth about a myth the people of the town have always believed and wonders what he should do. One of his friends advises him, "When the legend gets bigger than the truth, print the legend."

As far as the characters drawn from life in this novel go, I've been much more interested in the legend than in the truth. Even though many of these people lived, the versions of them that appear here are largely fictional. It is my hope that I've treated them fairly.

Michael Scott Cain is the author of seven books of poetry, most recently *East Point Poems*, and three novels, including *Midnight Train*, a country music novel. After teaching popular culture and literature at the collegiate level for forty years, he now covers the topic in *The Frederick News-Post* while also serving as jazz, blues, poetry, and folklore editor for *Rambles*. Cain's current project is a social history of Americana music called *The Americana Revolution*.